Interesting Tales
of
Other People's
Woe

By Damon Stewart

*May all your tales
be interesting
minus the woe*

ISBN: 1489561854
ISBN 13: 9781489561855
Library of Congress Control Number: 2013910768
CreateSpace Independent Publishing Platform, North Charleston, SC

Production and Oversight by Duncan Crary Communications.

CONTENTS

Déjà Vu You Too, Champ | *1*
(First appeared in Word Riot, 2004)

Time | *11*
(First appeared in Salvage, April 2005)

Shreds | *19*

Dirk Zeppelin | *25*
(First appeared in Big Toe Press, 2004)

Lost in the Static | *37*
(First appeared in Hobart, 2004)

Turning Dust | *53*
(First appeared in Amoskeag, 2006)

Jack and Diane | *63*

The Kindness of Strangers | *77*

Fall Harvest | *97*
(First appeared in Full Circle, 2003)

Vicious Ghosts | *109*
(First appeared in The Morpo Review, 1999)

St. John | *123*

Walking | *141*

Déjà Vu You Too, Champ

Reincarnation is crap.

That's a little harsh. I'm not saying it doesn't exist, trust me, it does. What I mean is that reincarnation is not what the popular mind has it to be: some sort of grand redemption for do-gooders and a cosmic dunce cap for those who do evil, doling out higher planes of existence for the former and new varieties of insect for the latter. Nope. Actually, it's just the simplest interpretation of the word. Perhaps "recycling" would be more apt. That is, reincarnation is a literal event—living life over and over again. And again. Etc.

Sorry if I seem a little jaded here, don't mean to be disrespectful about the Great Beyond and all that. But in my experience, it's just the same song on an endless loop. Maybe there's an enlightened individual out there who would tsk-tsk my ignorance about these things. Look, if you know of anyone who has a clue on what I'm doing wrong, please tell them to call me. I'll pay.

But let me apologize for just up and throwing that at you with no introduction. I've had a few cocktails here in this bar—did you know this was a bar seventy years ago too? Swanky joint back then, Bombay Gin martinis, Jameson Manhattans, Hedrick beer and French wine. Cost 25 cents a drink, which was a lot back then, but I'd sit and sip on a hot summer night and the ceiling fans would hiss and I'd just stare at my drink until someone sat next to me that I could talk to. So thanks, and next one's on me.

Anyway, there you go, the Big Answer, the 42 if you're a Doug Adam's fan. Sort of a letdown, I'm sure. But hey, you won't even know it when it happens-it'll be fresh every time. So you got that to look forward to.

That's a lot, trust me.

You see, the problem is that unlike you, I remember every past life I've had.

I don't go back to the beginning of man or anything like that. Near as I can tell, I winked into existence sometime in the late 1830's or early 1840's. It's vague, because for the first few births, I wasn't around that much. Instantly self-aware, but it's confusing the first few times out of the box. Born, died within days of a fever. Born, lived until one or two, died of diphtheria. Born, died of tuberculosis. Malaria. Whooping cough. Influenza.

Around the late 1850's, I made it as far as eight. I was born into a rather dour Kansas farm family. From day one I had memories of the previous lives, short as they may have been, but I thought that such recollections were normal. When I could talk, I would start reminiscing with my mother (Mom Number 7—"M7"), asking her questions like, "Where is my other mother?" or "Hey, that reminds me of the time I died choking in my own vomit," in matter-of-fact tones.

They eventually threw me out of the house, muttering things like "evil" and "demons." Religion and too many years living on the plains had warped their sense. Since it was in the dead of winter, I died of exposure sometime the next morning. Those plains. Trust me, they could use more roadside billboards. Like, one every ten feet. Liven the place up a bit. I'm not going back until they either bring in dirt and make some hills or paint the state some livelier color. All that flat. Ouch.

Shortly after that, I was born into a family that lived on a farm in northern Michigan, just outside of Traverse City. Mom8's name was Mary Constance Dunning. I always thought it was charming and would often refer to her by her whole name. Since I was five when I started doing it, she spanked me, but only a couple of times, and after a while she thought it was cute.

Anyway, M8 raised me after my father—F8, naturally—went off to fight in the Civil War and died. Not in battle, there's not even any indirect glory in my life; he caught smallpox at camp and was dead eight days after he joined up. Not there though, he managed to stagger home, collapse into a pile of hay in the barn for a rest, and stayed there for a Rest. Which reminds me, I thought I saw that guy in a St. Louis bar in the 1950's, but he looked different of course and even he didn't remember who he was, so it was hard to confirm. There was this vibe about him, and the guy in the bar kept rubbing his left ear with the knuckles of his right hand, an odd trait I'd only seen in F8. But you can't just run up and say, "Hey, are you my father from that farm in Michigan, back in 1864?" You get punched.

I hung in there awhile in that life. The next ten years were spent helping M8 on the farm, milking, splitting wood, scything wheat, shoveling cow poop, chicken poop, pig poop, sheep poop and dirt. Lots of dirt. I can't remember exactly why now, but it seemed I was always having to shovel dirt around, digging holes here, moving piles there. You folks have no idea how often people moved dirt back then. Lotsa dirt.

And those country meals. Contrary to what you might have heard about "old timey cookin'," all I can say is that M8 couldn't pick an apple off a tree without managing to make the thing bland or somehow underdone. Back then, a good meal was something burnt, with lots of salt. Corn whiskey to wash it down, or at least erase the memory of it.

When I was a tall, strapping lad of sixteen, I took off for the nearest city, Port Austin, to find a job. It wasn't hard, the place was still booming, having taken off during the Erie Canal days and maintaining a good port business even with the competition from the railroads. I got work in a foundry, tending to a pig iron bucket that ran along a waist-high horizontal bar and transported molten lead from the furnace into rough forms that, when filled and their contents cooled, made small right-angle bars for general household use.

I dunno. I guess there was a need.

So there I was, sweating for fourteen hours a day at 3 cents an hour. "The good old days." Let me point out one, of many, clear improvements in the human condition—child labor laws. Well, for those fortunate enough to have them. I guess most companies now just contract these things to other countries where they don't have such inconveniences. But out of sight, out of mind, right? It's a free country, you can get your slave labor anywhere you want but here, I guess. Me, I'd rob banks before doing that again. If some of those kids from Central America or Asia get the chance, they're gonna come over here looking to kick somebody's ass, but that's not my problem.

Another good thing, while I'm at it—OSHA. Safety requirements. Such as, let's say ... shields. Shields on things like, I don't know, how about for example on molten pig iron buckets, so that an exhausted, underpaid and distracted sixteen year old in Port Austin, Michigan doesn't one day bend over to pick up a piece of licorice, get bumped in the ass by the bucket and have its fiery cargo spill all over his head? And while I was running around screaming, just before I died, my boss—this guy named Erastus Mann—kept yelling at me to go outside so I wouldn't mess up his shop.

That hurt, and frankly, I'm still a little angry about the whole thing. Not as angry as I was, but back in 1932, before I totally lost it—I'll get to that in a minute—I looked up his descendants and found out they lived in Erie, PA. Took a train out there one day, found his great grandson's house, knocked on the door and when he answered I popped him on the nose. Vengeance, even twice removed, feels good.

I've done the research, was able to find my obit for that particular messy ending. I wasn't born again until four days later, in August of 1878, so I must have floated around in the ether for a while. I usually do, but it's all woozy and vague and I can never remember it very well, other than an impression of Styrofoam packing. You know, those giant, loose noodle-shaped things? Reminds me of death, that stuff.

Anyway, I was born the third son of seven children into a family in Boston. F9, Leopold Drumm, was a Presbyterian Minister (there's some sort of sick joke there, but I can't quite figure it out). M9, Lorella, was a community do-gooder who ran the church soup kitchen for the Knights of Labor and taught "Scientific Bible Study" class on Tuesday evenings to middle-class wives trying to reconcile their upbringing with their common sense.

The food was better, I figured that out right away. I kept complimenting M9 as soon as I could talk, so much so she got suspicious, thought I was being smart ("Have I told you how much I like this?" "Are you being a sass?" "No! —" "Whack" "Aaahh!"). She was a very, "spare the rod, spoil the child, beat the shit out of him, closer to God," sort of person. But I eventually got the hang of her, and was able to deflect most of the day's quota of beatings on my ignorant and amnesiac siblings.

The clothing was much more comfortable, though. Refined cotton—one of mankind's unsung heroic inventions (shoes, however, haven't gotten that much better in a hundred years, unless you include running shoes—truly the shodding of kings). The house was much cleaner than the farm or the closet-sized hovel I rented in Port Austin. Oddly enough, I had more body lice, which wasn't much fun. I kept asking M9 about that, until she took me to a Dr. Philmont Glenridge-Drucker, "Specialist of the Torso and the Humors." He actually had one of those thin, curly mustaches and a top hat like a cartoon bad guy. There's a reason why the image is associated with wickedness—that oily fucker put me in sheep dip. It killed the body lice alright, whilst singeing my skin and turning my fingernails and toenails to goo (FYI—it takes about eight weeks for those to grow back. You want to be told this, not learn it). I was sore for weeks, and of course the lice settled immediately back in, but I was smart enough not to complain to M9.

But I got used to the lice and lived a tolerable life, if a bit dull. I tended to be a bit heavy during that particular go-around, and slightly nearsighted to boot. That, by the way, was very annoying. Damn glasses gave me headaches.

Anyway, at sixteen I was apprenticed to a barrow-handler. This profession is no longer, but back in the day, wheelbarrows were a popular and handy item, used for construction, transport of children, livestock, packages, dirt (it was still being moved around a lot), drunks, other wheelbarrows and an endless list of other shit, including actual shit.

Much like the auto industry today, the component parts of wheelbarrows were made by small shops—wheels here, the basin there, and so on. The one I worked in, owned by a quiet man named Nelbert Fullows, specialized in the construction of the two long poles that supported the giant basin and functioned as the handles used for lifting. That's all we did. Four of us cut, sanded and painted wheelbarrow poles, eight sets a day. Nell had a good business, and he was pretty easy to work for. Personally, I think the man was stoned most of the time. He would go to the paint closet three or four times a day, shut the door and come out ten minutes later, eyes glazed and not say a word for hours, just work quietly on his poles. Mutter to himself a lot, in this high, strained voice. Since he neither brought to, nor retrieved anything from, the paint closet, I can't think what else he was doing in there.

Anyway, so I had this job and despite the paunch and the spectacles I got a girlfriend, Nancy, whom I married when I turned seventeen. F9 did the formalities, and it was a pretty good wedding; food, friends, even some booze that F9 and M9 pretended not to see in the back corner of the reception hall. Nelbert made me crew foreman afterwards and gave me a raise. Nancy's folks set us up in a nice house on Beacon Hill and I started leading a totally ordinary life. I almost forgot about the past-lives business, since after sixteen it was all new and I started hoping all the other stuff was some sort of dream. Nancy got pregnant, and nine months later had a baby boy. Nicholas.

She died during delivery. I still don't like to talk about it. Nancy. Never met anyone like her since.

I was a little freaked by Nick, he kept looking at me like he knew me. I wondered if maybe he was like me and remembered the past, maybe even met me, though I figured the odds of that were pretty long. Anyway, I did my best to raise him, but he got appendicitis when he was five and that was the end of him. I keep looking for him even now, but he doesn't even know who he is, and I'm not sure what I'd do if I found him. Probably get arrested as some sort of nutcase, trying to hug him and calling him son.

I was getting a bit distant from it all before this happened, it was getting hard to take things too seriously if you could always try again, no matter what. But then Nancy and Nick came and went, and there was no trying again there. I come back but (if you'll pardon the pun), I'll be damned if they can.

Sometimes I think that I keep coming back just so I can keep finding more to lose.

Anyway, Nell died in his sleep a year later. I'd be surprised if it didn't have something to do with all those paint fumes. So I took over the business. Did alright, too, doubled production to 16 sets a day (we saved time by not painting the "standard" models—only the "luxury" product got painted, a cheap green which allowed me a quadruple markup and a tidy profit on the high-end units).

Things were looking up again, until one night when I got drunk in the local tavern, walked outside to relieve myself, and started peeing on a horse. Trigger had a more refined sense of dignity than I thought, and the resulting kick put the lights out on Life Number 9.

Life Number 10 was very, very strange. First, there was a long time in the Styrofoam, almost twenty years, and then when I was born, I came back as a girl. Someone lost the instructions on the procedure, I think. I never got the hang of the dresses M10 kept putting me in, and going to the bathroom was a real bitch (turns out they really can't do it standing up, very messy). But overall I handled it with aplomb, if I may say so myself.

Then I turned twelve and the hormones kicked in. That totally fucked me up. I mean, I was miserable. Good looking, by the time I was seventeen I had this long black hair, a perfect figure with a decent rack and a great ass—shit, I took narcissism to a whole new level—but I was still miserable. Angry, depressed, even mildly hallucinatory at times. Left home at eighteen, worked in a sweat-shop in L.A. until I finally lost it one day, grabbed a Tommy-gun from a rum-running gangster friend and attacked a police barracks, figuring I'd end it all in a blaze of gunpowder and lead. Note to self—if I choose suicide-by-cop again, go after people who are good shots. I figured I'd hit a desk-cop or two, but assumed some street-wise veteran would take me out shortly thereafter. Turns out I mowed the whole place down and was beginning to think I'd have to find another and shoot slower. But a sergeant managed to pull his bullet-riddled body together for a final effort, got into a squad car and ran me over as I walked down the street. That hurt too, almost as bad as Port Austin.

Life 11 was another short one—died in a car accident on the way home from the hospital after delivery. I could see that F11 hadn't slept much and I was trying to tell him to stay awake, but even my screaming wasn't enough and he dozed the car into an oncoming milk truck.

L12 started in '48, and it was the best. I grew up in a small town in the Catskills. My folks were teachers who had a nice house in the village. I breezed through the first twenty years in paradise—the food just kept getting better, the clothes softer, the houses warmer, the girls easier—and went off to college in Vermont. I stayed out of the protest side of the '60's. I agreed with the ideas but based on what I've seen, people haven't changed all that much—those kids meant well but it all went to shit anyway. So I just went along for the drugs and sex, the former rather weak compared to nowadays, but the latter was fantastic and plentiful. I got drafted, figured that for once I'd see my end coming and wasn't as frightened as I was interested in the process. But I got assigned to a desk in New York, helping track ammunition shipments to Saigon. Did my stint and stayed in the city to enjoy the '70's. Now that was a decade. People talk about the sixties, but it was all so serious, really, you never found anyone with a sense of humor. In the '70's, it was all a joke and the laughing was perpetuated by copious amounts of quality amphetamines, cocaine, increasingly powerful marijuana and better acid.

I sold all of the above 'til '79, when I got busted. I was looking at some serious prison time, so for once this whole recycling deal proved handy and I used it to escape, if you know what I mean. Smoked a monster joint and went for a swim in the harbor.

So here I am in Life Number 13. I'm twenty years old, going on one hundred twenty, and, as I have recently been wondering, how do I get out of this?

Shit, how did I get into this? And why the 1830's or '40's? I did some research—well, paid some kid to research for me, actually—to find out if anything special happened back then. He gave me a long list of stuff but I only remember a few—the panic of 1837, the election and short, pneumatic tenure of William Henry Harrison ("Old Tippecanoe," I remember that for some reason), the Great Famine of Ireland.

Nothing stands out, although I do remember one date—April 23, 1843. That's the date that one William Miller predicted the Great Encore of Christ. Millerites—as the thousands that believed him were called—bought it hook, line and sinker. Sold their farms and got ready.

Whew—lots of disappointment on April 24th. I hate to be cruel, but April Fool's day comes a bit early, know what I mean? And wouldn't it be a kick if that was the day I was first born? No Savior—sorry folks, they sent me instead.

But shoot, maybe I've been around forever, maybe you have too. Supposedly we are all made of stardust. As in, the matter in our bodies is literally composed of the remains of exploded stars. But it's not my body that comes back, each one rots. I was tempted to dig one up once, see if anything hit me, any revelations, maybe get some form of closure on this, but I just can't quite get the motivation to go grave digging.

Every once in a while, when I'm sleeping, I'll have this dream—I'm on a horse, holding a sword, swinging into ... something, it's at night and there's a fire just off to my right but I can't see and people are screaming and the dream isn't that clear and I wake up feeling ... whatever. So there, maybe I'm cursed, maybe I ransacked a Cherokee village, chased the Mormons out of Cleveland or just got drunk and mad and cut down a church choir having a hoot turned horrible on a Saturday night.

Or maybe I watch too much TV these days (and I watch a lot, it has simply not lost its fascination for me).

My point: it's possible that some redemption is in order. I mean, even in the lives I remember, I've never done much for anyone else. I never saved anyone. Never helped anyone. Helped a few die.

No joy. No ... taking part in things. Just watching and either bitching or laughing. I need passion, I guess. I don't know, but I'm willing to try if it will end this cycle. I've had some good times, but that's not enough anymore. And I'm tired of poverty or a middle-class ceiling. Immortality without cash is like being confined to Disneyland, only you're prohibited from the rides and can only watch—interesting at first, a fade into boring, a freakish hell eventually.

But I did care for some people. Nancy. My son. F8, M12 and F12 meant something to me. During Life Number 12 I had a dog for two years, his name was Ozzie. That dog, I dunno. I started to connect again. With him, things began to feel real.

Word of advice my friend, apropos of nothing, but if you own a dog and wish to rid him of ticks? Rubbing alcohol works. So will a match. However, administration of rubbing alcohol followed by a match can have tragic consequences.

I once thought I heard a bark in the Styrofoam, but I never found him. Ol' Ozz.

Passion. Does it have to be for people or grand ideas? Will it suffice if I get passionate about stamp collecting? Polished gems? Country music? Perhaps roses? Or something obscure, something I can master, make a name for myself and perhaps inspire others.

Flame. That's it. I'll seek and photograph flames. I know they are different colors, depending on what's burning—beautiful alcohol blues, the ubiquitous wood yellows, metallic greens, and molten reds (that one I know very well). Flames. I can do a photo book, with the history of the flame. Little pop-culture sidebars, e.g. flame paint jobs on a motorcycle, flame tattoos, flame-broiled burgers and those Christmas video-flame fires. The flames of Hell.

I'll donate the proceeds to charity. UNICEF, the Salvation Army or the SPCA.

I know what you're thinking. I don't fear that. I don't. It's a change, and Lord (or the Closest Approximation Thereof) knows I need a change. Saying "I've faced death and it has made me stronger," is silly. That's just the problem. Death is like losing your first tooth, a bit painful, but you just keep tugging and there it is in your hand. The next one is always easier.

I don't need death. I need oblivion.

So here's what I'm doing: I've sort of put an order in, a message to the Man in Charge. I've had myself hypnotized, with a phrase burned into the tangled mass of neurons in my head. I'm hoping it'll stay with me, connect with that ethereal essence that's really me and allow me to inform whoever is making the casting decisions: I quit. Let's end this loop, or one last time, at the most.

I hope it wasn't a mistake. I'd hate to be in the Styrofoam for a few years with that echoing around in there, only to come back into L14 to still have it repeating the nine month ride in M14. I'd have to wait until I was old enough to have it hypnotized back out (it's not like I can go and have it done when I'm six, no one is going to do that to a little kid).

And I want to go out in style this time, do something unique. Inserting myself into a particle accelerator and getting zapped into another dimension sounds attractive, but a scientist friend of mine said that even if I managed to get near one, which was very unlikely, all it would do is give me a headache.

What I'd really like to do is shoot myself into space and let this body orbit the earth forever, sort of a monument to myself. That would make me famous, everybody would be talking about it. But I can't figure out a way to get up there.

Maybe I'll follow the lead of Frankenstein and the Eskimos—I'll get a flight to the Arctic Circle and wander off into the wasteland, maybe catch a ride on an iceberg into the great unknown. Take a nap somewhere and see if I wake up here again (note to myself—downside is the possibility of being reborn in the same area, which means a long walk to the beach). It'll give me some time to think, and will be a new experience, anyway. Or maybe I'll blow myself up, or leap into a volcano. If I do come back, it could give me ideas for my Flame coffee-table book. Just as long as it doesn't hurt too much. I never get used to that.

So time to get cracking, see if this will work.

If not, I have a back-up plan. No struggling through poverty again—I recently robbed a bank and used the proceeds to buy a life insurance policy. My beneficiary is my attorney, who is directed that upon my death ("accidental," of course) he is to put the proceeds into trust and wait eighteen years. Then he is to give the lot (minus a very generous cut to insure fidelity) to anyone who gives him the password. Someone who is, say, me, only in a different body. I'm not telling of course, but I won't forget it, right?

Drink up, I'll get us one more round. Here's to me, and wish me luck.

Time

The city bus shuddered and heaved its way over the car-eating potholes of Third Street, lumbering through the sleet like a tank in defiance of enemy fire. Burke sat in the back of the empty bus, staring out the window at half-remembered landmarks: Dence's Tavern, the house with the collapsing garage—still collapsing, after all these years, it surprised him—the pizza shop, only it was an empty storefront now, the "Pizza" lettering on the glass faded and peeling. About one more mile, he thought, and glanced down at his hands. He used to hold Jacquelyn's hand. Burke smiled, remembering how it felt.

His black coat radiated the smell of new leather, a gift from Sykes. He hoped it would make an impression on Jacquelyn. Burke stuck his hand into the left pocket of the coat, making sure it was still there—the other gift from Sykes.

He looked at his boots and pursed his lips. He had done his best to clean them, but they were creased and stained—hiking boots, comfortable if a bit worn down at the heels, and he didn't think anyone would notice that they were at least five years out of style—they all looked the same to him anyway. His jeans, one of the two pairs that he owned, were spotless. They were faded to a perfectly uniform robin's-egg blue, softness approaching that of silk. Not unique, nothing you'd necessarily remember, but nice nevertheless. He nodded in self-approval. He wanted to look good for Jacquelyn. He had a first impression—two actually—to make tonight, and one had to pay attention to details with these things.

He figured he had changed some. Probably thinner than when she last saw him, but no doubt in much better shape. He'd been exercising regularly for at least four years now. He used to have a ponytail—they called him "Whitetail," and smiled when they did—but it felt too suggestive of his past, too easy to mark him. So that morning he had walked into the first place he could find and instructed the girl to "make it short and something that looks... I dunno, current." She giggled, chewed her gum hard for a moment, then chopped it all off and charged him $20—for a haircut that, as near he could tell, was current when he was a small boy.

He reached into the green nylon duffel bag that sat next to him and pulled out a black baseball cap with "Lucky Duck" printed in yellow stitching above the brim. He had no clue what the hell it meant, but it only cost $2.50 and would serve its purpose well enough. He put it on, then took it off again, adjusting the plastic tab in the back. He placed it back on his head, pulling the brim down low and staring at his reflection in the window. Perfect. He stuck it back into the duffel.

There—they passed the old church with the giant red doors, the words "Church of the Redeemer" lit up above them. His stop was the next block. He stood, grabbing the duffle as he tapped the strip above the window. Burke heard the "ding" and clutched at a pole as the driver let off the gas. The bus lumbered to the curb and Burke stepped out of the rear door into a pile of slush, almost falling as the bus roared away in a blast of diesel.

Looking down the street, he saw the convenience store a few blocks away, a Fastmart. Burke looked around, DeLisle used to live near here, a couple of blocks back. Last month, when Burke was planning the trip, he considered looking DeLisle up to see if he wanted to do something. Then found out DeLisle was dead, some shit about killing his girlfriend in a fight and a subsequent suicide-by-cop. DeLisle didn't seem the type, but Burke was no longer surprised by anything.

No one on the street. There wouldn't be, it was a late weeknight and the weather was sufficiently rotten to discourage most from going out. Even the streetlights seemed muted, hunkered down against the sleet. Burke set the bag on the ground and unzipped it, pulling out the cap, a dark blue zip-front sweatshirt with a large hood, and a pair of gloves. The sweatshirt was also new but had a smell he didn't like, all plastic and chemicals. It was warm though, which was good, thought Burke. The wind drove the damp right into him. He quickly put the hat on, shrugged into the sweatshirt and gloves, then pulled the hood over his head, tightening the drawstring. Another quick look around and Burke started off, leaning into the wind and squinting. He patted the duffel bag again, checking for the hundredth time that the package was still in there. Sykes had told him to make sure to get her a gift.

"For two reasons, dude. A, you're supposed to, it's just what you do. B, it'll be awkward when you meet and this way she'll focus on the gift for a minute, let some of the weirdness bleed out of the room."

Burke figured Sykes had a point. It had been so long since he'd seen Jacquelyn—when they'd last been together she had to be pulled away from him, crying. He stopped his own tears—barely. Didn't tell her—barely—how much he'd miss her or how sorry he was. But he didn't want to give anyone the satisfaction of seeing him like that, so he had just walked away. Then the numbness set in. During the time they'd been apart, time itself had halved its progress, paradoxically leaving him with the feeling that twice as much was passing by in the rest of the world. He'd lost his sense of it, then lost care for it.

Burke didn't fool himself into thinking he would ever make it up to her; their separation had been too abrupt and too long. But he figured there would be some feelings remaining—had to be, it was the way of things.

"Time waits for no one, and it won't wait for me." Some song that Sykes always used to sing, the lines long since burned into his head. It wasn't a happy song, and Burke didn't particularly like it, but it usually surfaced into his consciousness at moments like these, when stress and possibilities loomed over him like waves, the trick being to hold his breath until the seas calmed again.

Two car-lengths from the Fastmart, Burke stopped, looking further down the street. A left at the next intersection, just past the store, led to Jacquelyn's house. It was down a steep hill, keep going and you got to the river; the Hudson looked slow but the current, especially this time of year, was strong. Jacquelyn was about halfway down on the right.

He walked to the other side of the street, and then back and forth past the Fastmart, thinking. If he blew this there wouldn't be another chance. But if it worked, it would give him something, the means to start over. Burke crossed the street again and went into the store. He got a cup of coffee, taking his time wandering through the aisles before throwing two dollars at the clerk on his way out, not waiting for change.

The frozen rain stung his face again as he crunched through broken ice towards Jacquelyn's house. As he approached he could see the blue glow from the TV illuminating the bay window in the living room. He hoped Jacquelyn's mother was in bed, but it was too early for that. She was probably sitting with Jacquelyn, watching TV, gently administering poison to Burke's character with off-the-cuff remarks and subtle suggestions. He had called Lori that morning to say he was coming, the first conversation they'd had in years. It hadn't gone any better than the last conversation they'd had.

He walked up the crumbling steps to her front door, then realized he hadn't even considered whether Lori had a husband or boyfriend—he hadn't heard of one, just assumed there weren't any. Could be difficulty if there were, but he'd deal with that as it came along. He took his sweatshirt and cap off, stuffing them back into the duffel with the gloves.

Lori answered the door on the third set of knocks. Burke was shocked; if he aged as much as she did, Jacquelyn wouldn't recognize him. She was still pretty, but so much older.

"Michael."

"Lori."

"You remember what I said on the phone, Michael—any shit, anything funny at all, and I call your parole officer. You got one hour."

"Yeah, I missed you too."

But she wasn't listening; she had turned away and was walking down a long, dark hallway. Burke followed, suddenly numb again, clutching the duffel bag containing the package tight against his chest.

"In there." Lori pointed to the room on her right, then at Burke. "One hour." And then down the hall into the kitchen.

Burke didn't mind. An hour was all he wanted, indeed all he had. Otherwise, he had the leverage to stay longer; hell he could move in. She didn't see it yet, that was clear, but he'd save that for later.

Burke hesitated at the threshold, then went in.

The lights were out and the volume on the TV was turned up too high; Burke frowned, he wanted to be able to see her, hear her, perfectly.

She was sitting on the couch, staring at the TV, her hands folded in her lap. He noticed her left foot shaking back and forth. I do the same thing when I'm nervous, he thought, and grinned. Then frowned again; he wished this weren't something that made her nervous.

He cleared his throat and she turned to him.

"Daddy." She smiled, waved at him then stared back at the TV.

14

Sykes had said this was the time to give her the package, get her attention off of him. But it already was and Burke didn't know what to do.

"Hey Jacquelyn. I got something here for you." Burke unzipped the duffel and pulled out a box. He walked over to the girl and sat down next to her on the couch.

"Here."

She grabbed the box without taking her eyes off the TV, some cartoon, a talking sponge or something. She ripped the paper off the box, felt around the edges then moved her hands towards the center. When she got to the plastic window, she looked down.

"Barbie."

"You like it?"

"I got that one already," and Burke felt the frustration like an old wound, so familiar that he wasn't sure if it even hurt anymore. She suddenly looked up at Burke, reached over and gave him a quick kiss on the cheek.

"Thanks, Daddy."

Not knowing what else to do, Burke sat back and watched the cartoon in silence with her. After a minute, she grabbed his hand and held it. Her hand was big enough to grasp four fingers; she didn't have to just grab one anymore. That did it, and Burke had to look away towards the hall for a moment.

"So. How's school?" during a commercial.

"Fine."

"What grade you in?"

"Second."

Her attention was on the show, so he waited for the next commercial before resuming their catching up.

"Play a lot of games?"

"No."

Lori walked by, scowling into the room. Jacquelyn looked at her mother as she passed, then at Burke.

"I don't think she likes you."

Burke smiled. "Nope."

"Do you like her?"

"I like you," he said, and they returned to the TV.

They sat there for the next twenty minutes, watching the animated adventures of happy creatures. Once, Burke thought, he had plans for when he got out, a new start, legit this time, find some nine to five minimum-wage ex-con job and glide away the days in poverty and peace of mind.

But no. He had ambition, of sorts.

"Michael. Time. Leave." Lori's glaring eyes from the doorway, the shadows from the talking sponge blinking across her face.

Burke turned to the girl.

"Sweetie, how long do you think I was here?"

"I don't know."

"Two hours?"

"I guess," in that TV-watching monotone; as if the effort of tone or pitch would throw off understanding of the plot.

"So I was here for two hours?"

"Um-hmm."

"I'm not going to see you again for a while, ok? I have to go visit some friends. But I'll come back, I promise. Alright?"

"Ok, Daddy." The show went to commercial, white light filling the room, and Burke saw her face, blank, and he thought he could see in her the numbness he felt. He knew how it got there, and was surprised by his culpability. Never say never, he thought.

"Gotta go honey. Give me a kiss?"

She leaned over and kissed him on the cheek. "Bye, daddy."

"Bye, Jacquelyn."

Burke got up and walked past Lori, who was staring over his shoulder.

At the door, Burke turned around. "They wanted to know who drove."

She turned to face him.

"I coulda got less time. They offered a deal."

She looked at the floor.

"But I shut up. My lawyer told me I was nuts. Did a lotta years, just two words was all I had to say. Lotta years, Lori."

Something appeared to occur to her and she looked up again sharply.

"So what do you want?"

"I was here for two hours. Got here at 10:00, like I did, but didn't leave 'til midnight. But only if anyone asks." Burke paused. "Got it?"

"Fuck you." He could see her steeling herself, ready for a confrontation. Ready—hoping, he was sure—to call the cops, but he wouldn't give it to her that easy.

"Two things, Lori. One. Don't know if the statute of limitations has passed on all that. Maybe. Maybe not. You want me to ask the cops to check? They will. You're unfinished business; that don't work, they'll find something else, you know?"

The eyes. She remained erect, jaw up, body tense. But the eyes, the lines around them softening perhaps, just a bit, but enough to see that he had hit.

"Two. I bet the 'something else' they find is her," and he nodded down the hall past Lori. "Social services finds out, they'll want to know all about you. You a good mom, Lori? Got the money to prove it in court?"

Burke didn't have a clue if social services would care or not, but she shifted her eyes to look past him out the door, and he saw her shoulders sag.

"So, let's do this one more time: I was here for two hours. Got it?"

"Yeah. I got it." She opened her mouth again, he could see the question coming and shook his head. She looked back down at the floor.

Outside, he paused at the doorstep. Further down the hill was the stop for the return bus. It wasn't too late, he could bail out now and take the bus to the homeless shelter. Spend the night and figure something out in the morning.

Up the hill, he could see the lights of the Fastmart.

Stick to the plan, he thought, all I need is a start. He opened the duffel and pulled out the sweatshirt, hat and gloves. Before putting on the sweatshirt he reached into the pocket of his coat and retrieved the .38, quickly shoving it into the pocket of his sweatshirt. A friend of Sykes', on the outside, owed Sykes. And Sykes owed Burke, who had once come across Sykes in the prison shop, on his back with another man's knee on his chest and a sharpened screwdriver in Sykes' ear, ready to permanently loosen an essential screw. Burke had inserted the screwdriver in its owner's thigh instead. And thus the gun, and anything else Burke ever needed that Sykes could provide.

He walked up the slope towards the light of the Fastmart, tugging his cap low against the wind, rain and facial features; pulling the hood over his head to obscure his height. Both, along with the gloves, to be ditched in the river.

He had the layout: a surveillance camera in the far corner above the cooler, another on the wall behind the register. Clerk was some bored girl, the place closed up in ten minutes; she wouldn't be trouble. No one on the street, no one in the store, wait if there was. Front door four steps from the register. Lay low somewhere, somebody's garage, an unlocked car or back porch, 'til morning. The duffel held a tightly packed sleeping bag. They'd check hotels, but wouldn't consider anyone staying out in this shit.

Then the bus to the college across town; weeks earlier Burke had answered an ad from a student looking for someone to split the gas money and the driving down to North Carolina on break. Sykes had taught him that trick, no suspicious cops at the bus or train station to hassle with. He said a guy with a little cash could get himself a good start down in North Carolina, even had some friends who'd help him out.

Burke took a breath and started up the hill.

It was time.

Shreds

Herrick was walking down a busy street in Tongbai. He strode with purpose, lost to the city's sights and sounds. He didn't care. It wasn't famous for anything that Herrick was aware of, indeed he'd never heard of the place until he had stomped off the train and saw the sign on the platform.

He was alone, intentionally so. He was cold, which was more of an accident because in his haste to depart the train he had forgotten his coat, and winter in central China required a coat. Preferably a hat and gloves as well, both of which were also now chugging down the line without him.

He'd been traveling the past couple of days with Reynolds and Lisa, the latter for whom he had harbored an attraction the entire semester. Ever since they had planned the trip together—as friends, nothing more—he had been hoping that they'd hook up, but it was spoiled by Reynolds tagging along at the last minute.

Reynolds' presence wasn't a complete obstacle per se, just a hindrance. Or so he first thought when Reynolds walked into his room and asked to come along. Herrick, who had been packing the last of his things and preparing his good-byes, thought he was joking. But Lisa, who was also in the room, was nodding her head in agreement before Reynolds finished the question. Herrick knew, with a sinking feeling, that he'd look petulant or manipulating by objecting. Technically, Reynolds didn't even ask him, as he was looking at Lisa the whole time anyway.

They had left Beijing the next day, choosing to travel by rail on a zigzag route south to Hong Kong for the return flight home. First to Xian, where they toured the dusty tomb of a stone army and listened to Reynolds, a history major, explain their significance. Supposedly to both of them but again only looking at Lisa.

They had finished by noon and next stop was Nanjing. But since their train didn't leave Xian until late afternoon, they spent the intervening hours in a ramshackle bar half a mile from the station, drinking cheap Yungang beer and listening to Reynolds tell stories about the summer he and some friends had formed a band and toured Texas. Herrick was alternatively bored and annoyed, the latter at Reynolds' obvious exaggerations—there was no way they opened for Everclear—but Lisa seemed to be enraptured. Herrick, observing the signs, became quietly frantic, wishing to interrupt Reynolds' rhythm or orchestrate his departure, alive or dead. But there was nothing he could do but listen and wait for the clock to break the spell and direct them to the train.

Once aboard, it only took two hours for Reynolds to quite simply, and literally, charm the pants off of Lisa. After stumbling into their compartment—although for all his seeming stagger, Reynolds quite nimbly got the seat next to Lisa, forcing Herrick to the opposite side—Reynolds began again with more stories and jokes, making her laugh and ask for more. He got her to talk about herself, personal things. Herrick thought the questions were bold, offensive even, quite personal in nature. But she talked at length about a prior boyfriend, a friend's drug problem, and her parents' divorce. All the while sharing her gaze more and more with Reynolds, seeming to forget Herrick's presence, even though he offered noises of sympathy and encouragement.

Reynolds had soon sidled thigh to thigh with Lisa, and, with Herrick watching, he did it, made the 'ol stretch-and-put-arm-over-her-head move, so contrived and stupid Herrick almost smiled in expectation of Reynolds' imminent rejection and embarrassment.

Nothing of the sort. Lisa responded by snuggling a little closer, and closing her eyes with a dramatic sigh. Reynolds looked at Herrick, the message clear—please go to the bathroom, for a walk, throw yourself out the window if necessary—but just leave. Herrick affected ignorance, smiled and nodded at Reynolds, hoping to interrupt the thickening of the bond between the two long enough to think of something; yell fire or arrange Reynolds' kidnapping. Buy some more time so he could get her to notice him again, just let her focus on him for a few minutes, bring her back to where they were before Reynolds tagged along.

I didn't even slow the bastard down, Herrick reflected as he trudged over the cracked pavement of the street, stepping over random chunks of stone, trash, and the occasional weary soul too tired, apparently, to find a suitable resting place. Reynolds had just turned to Lisa and whispered something in her ear. She giggled—giggled for Christ's sake—then said, "Jon, would you mind ... sort of ... maybe taking a walk? I'm sorry," and she shook her head, her serious, brown eyes sorry indeed, until Reynolds slipped his hand underneath her shirt and started rubbing her back, causing her to turn to him and give him a halfhearted slap. "Wait," she said sharply, but then gave him such a radiant smile, touching his cheek and whispering again, "wait," her tone promising so much more than permission to rub her back, that Herrick lost all fight and left without a word.

Walked straight to the bar car and drank three beers over the ensuing forty minutes, until the train stopped at Tongbai Station. Looking through the windows opposite him, Herrick could see the smog nestled firmly over the gray one and two story concrete buildings, mud and broken gravel decorating a dilapidated road, faceless people in varying states of sartorial poverty shambling about under the darkening sky.

He abruptly stood, chugged the remains of the Yuangang, and marched straight off the train into the gloom of the crude concrete platform. Not a second thought, just a steady, dull anger and frustration to propel him forward. To what, exactly, wasn't even the point.

He walked through the city for an hour, not seeing anything around him as he moved randomly through the streets, his breath just visible in angry white gusts, hands jammed into the pockets of his jeans, the hood of his sweatshirt pulled over his head. He didn't need his luggage, but he wished he brought his coat.

She had been so nice to him all semester. He knew that didn't mean shit, but she really seemed to like him, and when she agreed to take the trip with him, he thought that maybe she saw signs of a relationship. He wasn't expecting to sleep with her, just hoping for the chance to get closer, get that connection, then see if they could take it another level when they got back to Ithaca.

He should have seen it. She was like Diane, wanted him close, closer than the rest, but not that close, saving the final space for someone else. He'd get over it. He'd done it before, but how much was he supposed to take?

He could handle a lot, more than most, or at least he had the experience to back up the claim. His father died suddenly when he was thirteen; a cardiac arrest, in bed with the neighbor's wife, who was also the mother of his best friend. He took it, though, didn't immediately run off the teenage rails, just staggered a bit under the weight of the grief and kept going. His mother, family, friends, the school therapist, all remarking on how well he absorbed the blow. "So well-adjusted, such a nice young man," they said. They were right, he knew it. It was what he had to do.

Later, the summer before his senior year, he handled the car crash and DWI well, too. A guilty plea and a public apology in the school auditorium to the girl whose back got broken (long rehab, some lifelong discomfort, but not quite crippled). He gave the family what was left of his father's inheritance. The girl didn't sue, it was agreed to be a youthful, tragic mistake, but he paid what he could anyway, because there was nothing else he could do.

He took the beating the girl's brother and father administered one Saturday night, admitted he deserved it and didn't call the police, insisting to his mother that he had simply fallen down some stairs. Lots of them, and twice. She knew better, and he took her frustration and sorrow over her battered son like he'd taken everything else.

And after his thirty days in county jail, he took it when he learned that his college of choice—and apparently all others—would no longer accept him. So he got a pizza delivery job, dropping off dinners to the embarrassed families of former classmates, and when necessary, acknowledged the reason why he was there without any hesitation.

But two years later, he finally did get to school—Ithaca College, making everyone proud—and he started over again. He met Diane, his life started changing, turning into what he wanted it to be. But nothing dramatic happened, comparatively speaking, she just met someone else, some guy from back home, some guy who happened to be, at the time of their final discussion, the father of her baby.

He almost broke then, almost let the rage out, but he reined it in. Expressed his sorrow for his loss, his wishes for her and her baby's luck, and offering help if she ever needed it, not even completely insincere. He'd handled so much else, he could handle that too.

But she didn't need his help. She left, and he had to move. California was his first choice, but his mother, begging, convinced him to stay in school, let the school move with him if he was that restless, and so he chose a semester abroad. Beijing, China, as far as he could go.

Kept to himself at first, but as the weeks passed, he started to give, let the environment pull him in. It was all new, no one knew him or cared, he was a clean slate again. It was late in the semester by the time he realized this, but Herrick decided to make the best of it with the time he had. Realized that Lisa seemed to like him, and decided to do something about it. The result was planning their little sightseeing tour together.

And he was now walking through Tongbai by himself.

There was no real crisis, he knew, taking a deep breath and calming down for the first time. He didn't have a coat or his luggage, but angry and impulsive as he was, he had walked off the train with his wallet, which contained $400 yuan, $800 in Traveler's checks, and his mother's somewhat limited Visa card for emergencies. This, he decided, qualified.

He saw a small shop across the street to his right, with people walking out holding steaming cups, and he stopped. Crossed the street and went in, coming out a moment later with a cup of hot green tea. He started forward again, more slowly, planning the rest of the way to Nanjing. He, Lisa and Reynolds had planned to stay at the Jinling Hotel for a few days; all he had to do was catch the next train and meet them there. They would take care of his things. He'd have a drink with the two of them, say what had to be said, and part ways as gracefully as possible, get back home and start again.

Suddenly he noticed a commotion ahead. There was a boy, early teens, standing on the sidewalk, his back to a crumbling brick wall. The boy was crying—if that was the word, Herrick thought. He was ... weeping, raging actually, his tears flowing down his red, contorted face as he stood on the street and shredded a small fistful of yuan notes.

The kid was wearing cheap sandals, soles made of recycled tires, ill-fitting and not nearly enough for the cold. Ripped and stained pants, his dirty long underwear visible through the torn clothing. Ragged shirt, nylon vest, coat, all equally in disrepair, worn in a way suggesting a permanent condition.

Herrick was stunned—he had a taste of hard times, it was tough for a while after his father had died, but even that hardship was almost embarrassingly luxurious compared to most here. Certainly compared to this kid. But he felt it, whatever it was. It was deep and irrevocable, and Herrick just knew, by the way the boy stood there, oblivious to all with his abandoned keen, that there was nothing in the world that could help him. Whatever made him stand there, ripping up money—and Herrick was sure that kid was someone who knew intimately, painfully, the value of those shredded notes—it was beyond recall or redemption. It was Bad, and it was Done.

He couldn't help him, which didn't stop him from trying, handing the boy 100 yuan. The kid didn't even stop to acknowledge it, just grabbed it, tore it up and stomped on it, not even looking at Herrick, just staring out into the street at his own private horror. Herrick felt it again, closer, the vibe: it was the one that he felt when he overheard his mother telling his aunt how his father died.

Some things you can't change. Herrick shrugged and walked on into the darkness, heading back to the station, ready to buy a ticket and get along down the line. It was what you had to do; push past these manifestations of sorrow and keep moving. In a way, he took all this too, took it for the kid. Herrick hoped the kid might notice and learn.

Dirk Zeppelin

"You're a what?" the girl asked, her bleary eyes searching Dirk's face. She hiccuped, then reached to the bar to clutch a glass of beer for support.

"A Dirigible Engineer," he replied, slower this time, raising his eyebrows in a way that added gravity to the title. Or so he hoped.

"A dirger-what?" she asked again, leaning forward to look fuzzily at his mouth.

"You know, at the arena?" Dirk asked, "during intermission in the hockey game? The dirigible, the big—"

From behind her appeared a form, an aggressively round protrusion that resolved into a belly, followed by the body of a man who chuckled and said, "He's a freakin' miniature blimp operator, sweetie."

Dirk scowled at the appearance of his arch-nemesis (his friend Lance's term, not his) and fellow employee of the Fort Orange Arena. The girl, who had taken another completely unnecessary swig of beer, sprayed it all over Dirk's lap as she laughed. The man grinned and looked at Dirk, displaying a mouthful of yellow teeth. "Hey, she got that on the first try, Dirkie."

"Screw you, Brett," said Dirk, looking around for a napkin to remove beer mist from his face. He picked one off the bar, but the girl grabbed it and blew her nose into it.

"Wanna go outside, cowboy?" and the belly took a step closer to Dirk.

Dirk, five feet six inches, one hundred thirty-five pounds if he ate a few tacos first, was not, despite the intensity of his glare, a match for the belly's owner. But he wondered if he could get a punch in and split before he was mashed. It might be worth a shot at that hated stomach, which was now poking out between the bottom of Brett's dirty T-shirt and top of his filthy jeans. Its one eye, cast in hairy malevolence, offered a baleful glare at Dirk, as if daring him to take up the challenge.

Brett closed his right hand into a toaster-sized fist; with the left he lifted his shirt and began to caress his belly, circling slowly towards center. The motion seemed both obscene and frightening. To attack the stomach, Dirk felt, would be to strike a blow for all that was good and decent. But as Brett's finger slipped into the void of that hell's outermost ring to retrieve a piece of damp lint, Dirk felt the belly and its master stare him down.

Then Brett shook his head and stepped back. "You ain't worth the trouble," and he turned to the bartender, who had just appeared before them with the air of a man about to intervene in other people's problems. "Gimme a Bud, a shot of Peppermint Schnapps, and another of whatever the lady here is drinkin'." He waited a beat, then, "Oh yeah, and a set of balls for this one," and jerked his head at Dirk. Brett threw a twenty at the bartender, "Keep the change," and turned to address the girl.

"Babycakes," he said, "I'm sitting over there," pointing to a corner of the bar, "and if you want to talk to a real man, come on over. Dirk—tell her what I do." With that, he turned and walked away.

"Well?" asked the girl, apparently oblivious of the passing rumble of potential violence. "What does he do? Is he a dirger ... dirger ... blimp-man too?"

Dirk hated this part. One day, he thought, Brett and his belly were going to pay oh so dearly, so keenly, and he nodded to himself in anticipation of self-righteous vengeance. This was the third time Brett had done this to him.

"He drives a Zamboni," Dirk said in an even tone that was supposed to suggest that not only was it not a big deal, it was no deal. A negative deal.

The girl squealed. "Ohmygod, you mean the ice machine? Do you think he'd let me ride on it?" and she turned to the corner where Brett was now sitting.

"I dunno. He's maintenance, I'm talent. I don't care what he thinks." Dirk took a sip of his beer, stalling while thinking of something to get that look out of her eye. "He might, I guess, since I think his probation's run out. But the last woman who did that—" and he stopped. The girl wasn't listening, she was twisted around on her stool, searching the corner for Brett. As if on cue, Brett stood up and showed his teeth in what might euphemistically be called a smile, making Dirk and the stranger next to him wince, and waved her over.

Without another word, the girl slid off her stool, bumped into a waitress carrying a tray of drinks, and wobbled over to Brett's open arms.

✶ ✶ ✶

The Fort Orange Arena could fit 17,000 people. On a good night, there might be 700 present to watch the city's minor-league hockey team, the "Feral Moles," whack away at a plastic disk for several hours against a team from some similarly godforsaken city that half the crowd had never heard of. For the Moles, victory was so rare as to be forgotten as the ostensible goal. For most fans, the purpose of attending was like watching a favorite episode of an old sitcom, its ending already known but new and amusing nuances to be explored in every additional viewing.

Dirk typically stood behind a low wall at one end of the rink, near the utility area where he could watch the action and be ready when his time came. During the breaks in play, his job—his performance—was to send a remote-controlled balloon (the size of a good sturdy couch) up and over the crowd, easing down now and then to drop coupons for free oil changes, buy-one-get-one-free pizzas, and trial memberships for health clubs. They would flutter into the waiting arms of happy fans who wouldn't actually use any of them, except for the pizzas, but all of whom felt a certain kind of low-level specialness at getting something for free.

The blimp—or "dirigible," as Dirk would insist to anyone for as long as required—until the universe stopped expanding if necessary—was a fairly new one, an "Airshark Mark II" with long-range radio control, a multi-directional micromotor turbofan propulsion system, and a 5 pound payload capability. Left to itself, the dirigible would gently float to the ground, but the mini fans were capable of moving it smartly about at a speed of about ten mph, as high as the rafters of the arena. Its titanium frame was encased in a polyurethane skin, painted black with the logo of a sneering green mole on the side.

Dirk had been working in the maintenance at the arena for a couple of years, performing odd jobs such as scrubbing gum from underneath seats, polishing floors and spiffying rest rooms until two months ago when he went to the management with a plan for a new form of entertainment. The previous act, a team of seven giant frogs that would hop onto a variety of colorful platforms that emitted a particular tone when landed upon, was no longer available (the key to that show was not so much time spent training frogs as it was utilizing a froggy form of amphetamine that got them to jump when lightly nudged. But the trainer one night accidentally mixed too much of the special sauce into their water right before they were on, only to have them hop insanely from platform to platform in giant, suicidal leaps that twisted "My Country, 'Tis of Thee," into a sort of rapid evil-circus music. It ended only when the last frog expired with a wet thump on the ice in front of the horrified crowd). For Dirk, it was a golden opportunity that launched a career.

Dirk left the bar and arrived at the indoor utility garage fifteen minutes before the game was to begin. The dirigible sat lightly on a pair of sawhorses, tethered to a scarred red canister of helium. Tonight's drop consisted of coupons for a carpet cleaning, a tooth-whitening system, and six-months of pet health insurance. Dirk clipped the packets of brightly colored paper to the plastic tongs that hung from the blimp's frame, checked the batteries and gave it a rough tug to test the buoyancy. Satisfied, he pulled it out by its leash and brought it over to the edge of the rink, gently pushing it backwards into a service corridor underneath the first row of seats. He glanced around for Brett, who usually brought the Zamboni up to the edge of the rink and watched while the machine's engine idled along, gently sputtering toxic fumes laced with the smoke from the cigar that Brett wasn't supposed to be smoking.

Brett was leaning against the Zamboni, parked a few feet away, talking to the girl from the bar with his arms around her. Dirk shook his head in a mixture of chagrin and disgust as he watched Brett grope her buttocks, squeezing away as though her buns were stress balls and he was having a particularly difficult day. Brett saw him staring and bent his head to say something into her ear. She started laughing and turned around to look in his direction; not directly at Dirk, but at the corridor where the dirigible sat waiting. Suddenly Dirk understood what they were laughing at. His eyes narrowed and he flushed, turning back to watch the players warm up while muttering to himself.

The front of the dirigible was a source of deep humiliation to Dirk. Right after acquiring the blimp, the arena's in-house painter had spent an afternoon getting the hockey team's logo on each side: a crouching, snarling mole holding a hockey stick in a way that suggested mortal combat as opposed to sport. It looked pretty cool as far as Dirk was concerned, but there was one more touch that he felt would complete the look and create a sort of low-rider of airships.

"No way Dirk, it'll look silly," said Benji the painter, "I'm telling you it won't end up looking like you think it will. Plus, I'm only supposed to paint the approved logo, and a skull head mole is not on the approved logo list."

"But—"

"Bye, Dirk," and he walked away.

When Dirk explained his dilemma to Lance, his more or less best friend (depending on how much weed and spending money Dirk had on him), Lance said, "Dude, we can handle this ourselves. I'm an artistic man, so are you. Let's just paint the fucker on there ourselves, when the boss sees it he'll love it. Maybe we'll get royalties for the new look, you know?"

A mixture of marijuana and cheap beer propelled them into the arena later that night, armed with several colors of spray paint and a design drawn on a torn napkin. The aforementioned chemical cocktail did not, as romantic lore would suggest, enhance or even bring out their (highly speculative) creative talents, and its effect on their motor function was worse. Their vision, such as it was, dissipated as day and sobriety approached; by dawn they threw up their hands and fell asleep in the player's lounge.

The end result, shown to an annoyed marketing manager named Arnie later that morning, was a blimp with face that looked not like a demon-mole come to lay waste to his hockey foes, but rather, depending on how one viewed it, a reasonable imitation of a festering sore or a rotted pig's head. If more people had opined "rotted pig's head" (the entire marketing staff was brought in for a viewing), Dirk might have salvaged some pride, but "festering sore," although expressed in various ways, seemed to be the consensus.

Dirk was reprimanded for "unauthorized modification" of company property, and Benji was called over to remedy the situation.

"Oh Jesus, no," said Dirk when Benji showed him the results.

"Listen Dirk, I don't have a lot of time and this takes care of the problem."

"But for Christ's sake Benji, how's that gonna scare anyone? It'll demoralize the team! The other side will laugh!"

"Maybe they'll get laughing so hard we can score some goals," said Benji, tapping his forehead as he walked away.

Benji had pragmatically chosen to emphasize the rotted pig's head perspective, and managed to heal the swine, indeed make it a chipper happy pig, with a big smile and winking eye.

"But what's a pig got to do with the Feral Moles?" Dirk later asked Arnie, who had been in the midst of trying to design an advertising campaign around a team that recently set a record for fighting—with each other.

"Dirk—listen—don't know, don't care. Just don't paint anything again, and don't bug me anymore."

"But—"

"Dirk," in a sharp voice that implied cessation of steady pay.

"Yes?"

"Don't."

The game proceeded and Dirk soon forgot Brett's slights. He got caught up in the action despite the inevitability of the outcome; tonight's false hope coming from a Feral Mole who tripped over his stick and accidentally kicked the puck into the goal. It didn't give them a lead or even a tie, but it was a goal, damn it, proof that it's not over until it's over. By the first intermission Dirk was cheering like a real fan as the teams filed into the locker rooms, almost forgetting that he had a job to do.

He got a helpful reminder from Brett: "Hey blimpie-boy, time to fly your loser kite," and a cigar butt flew past his ear.

Ignoring him, Dirk brought the dirigible out, untied the line and started the motors with the remote. The airship rose gently, and Dirk guided it over the wall, directing its ascent over the center of the rink.

This was the essence of the task for Dirk, as the effect of the balloon's initial appearance never failed to bring about a peculiar feeling in him, an essential calm suffused with a sense of accomplishment and possibility, the past no longer relevant and the future to begin on some undefined date, where he'd move beyond all this.

The crowd went silent as turning heads got the attention of other heads, forming a human wave of sorts, only this a sitting wave of attention, the focus on an extension of Dirk.

It only lasted a few moments, then the adults went back to talking amongst themselves, going to the bathroom or for food. Next came the teenagers, who soon got restless and began milling around, then the nine to twelvers began to fidget—but not the little kids, they remained seated, mouths open, staring in awed wonder as the Airshark Mark II glided silently through the arena's stratosphere.

Dirk cranked a tiny wheel on the remote and sent the balloon into a gentle descent towards the opposite corner. Down it went, regaining the attention of the people in reverse order, until the teenagers were elbowing their parents and pointing at the giant thing with the fierce mole painted on its side (and inexplicably gentle pig on the front) heading their way. Soon the whole section of seats was looking up and Dirk hit the release switch, sending tiny paper bombs of free products and services into their waiting arms.

Dirk guided the dirigible back towards his end of the arena; he liked to crisscross the space to keep the crowd interested. As he scanned the audience, he suddenly stopped to stare intently, high in the stands to his left.

She was in section G, up near the 110 level seats—long reddish hair pulled into a ponytail that revealed a face that had remained unchanged since high school, actually junior high, one that still brought about a tingling in his abdomen and a shock down to his knees.

When Dirk had been in seventh grade, lost in the crush of new kids and an unshakable reputation as being weird and thus one-to-be-occasionally-assaulted, Kelly Kraus sat next to him in study hall. She inhabited that space he aspired to, a land of happy kids with nice clothes and some money, pretty girls and music—well, he'd keep his own rockin' music, but still.

But Kelly didn't move to sit with her friends on the first day. Instead, she smiled at Dirk, asked him what he thought of Mrs. Fisher's math class, and spent the rest of the study-hall year chatting with him. Her friends didn't seem to notice; his refused to believe she legitimately interacted with him until a good month went by with no evidence of bribery or a cruel joke being played on one of their smitten fellow-peons.

It never developed into anything, but Dirk and Kelly were friends—at least for the next two years, during which she would sit next to him whenever they shared a study hall or occasionally walk with him to a class. Then she moved to a different school, and Dirk only heard about her once in a while or caught a rare glimpse at the mall. But that's all it took for Dirk, she became the Girl, the One, and at 24 he would still occasionally think of her in the "what if" way.

Without thinking, Dirk steered the dirigible towards her, smiling as a child of no more than two or three tugged at her sleeve and pointed to the approaching balloon.

Dirk brought it down low, only ten feet above her, and managed to make it wiggle from side to side in imitation of a fighter aircraft's "hello," although it could also be said to resemble a jolly pig lolling in his natural element. He could see her looking around for the dirigible's operator. Dirk first made sure his baseball cap was on backwards, set just so over his ponytail, that the stain on his Judas Priest tee shirt was covered by his arena employee badge (some might think it odd, clipped to his stomach like that, but it was the lesser of evils), and that his fly was firmly secured at its zenith. He then leaned over the rink wall and waved at her. After a moment she saw him. There was a brief pause, and then he saw the flash of recognition on her face.

"Hi Kelly," he mouthed, and pointed up. She looked at the balloon, and Dirk hit a switch and unloaded $80 worth of Dr. Doolittle's Pet Care Guarantee (six months, dogs and cats only, no fish, birds or rodents).

Deep in the lizard part of his brain, Dirk fully expected this to lead to nothing less than wanton sex underneath the bleachers. Or, at least, stunned appreciation leading to a date. Never mind the child or the obvious existence of a mate; Lizard Dirk just assumed that his prowess with machines of flight and his ability to unleash economic boon would render her senseless before him, flush with appreciation of his powers.

Even as lizard-brains go, Dirk's was unusually optimistic in its reptilian outlook and often had too much influence on his human thought processes.

A small shower of garishly colored coupons descended upon her. Her son, a blond haired boy with a bright purple "Handy Manny" sweatshirt, tried to grab one of the falling coupons and tripped over the back of the seat in front of him. He fell into the lap of the man in the seat, sending the man's sauerkraut encrusted hot dog into the hair of the woman in front of them. The boy started howling, the woman began yelling, the man stood up looking very annoyed, and Kelly, glaring at Dirk, stepped down over the two rows of seats to retrieve her son before marching up the stairs towards the exit.

"Oh crap," said Dirk, who then felt a hand clamp on the back of his neck.

"Way to go, fucko, see you impressed the ladies with that thing again, didn'cha?" said Brett, his breath smelling of the pickled eggs he kept in a jar underneath the Zamboni's seat.

Dirk yanked away, the motion inadvertently sending the blimp straight towards Kelly, who, turning around to see it in chase, started to run up the stairs, her look of anger transitioning into fear, visible even from where Dirk stood. He quickly reversed the blimp, sending it high towards the rafters before turning back to deal with Brett.

"Listen, you miserable bastard…" said Dirk. His anger at blowing what seemed to be a golden opportunity with Kelly had momentarily surpassed any rational calculation of his chances in battle.

"Yeah? You wanna step outside?" Brett asked, and he shifted his considerable bulk towards Dirk, bumping him with the loathsome gastric organ. It was his first actual contact with the belly, which Dirk thought surprisingly firm, suggesting massive amounts of muscle buried underneath. Needed, no doubt, so as to move it about from pickle jar to hamburger joint.

Dirk reconsidered. A confrontation with Brett would require him to either leave the blimp floating about the arena on its own, guaranteed disaster, or telling Brett to wait the several minutes it would take to bring it back to be tied up, and then to go outside and get his ass kicked.

Dirk looked down and said, "Go fuck off, Brett. Don't you need to play on the ice?"

"You got it, sonny boy," poking his finger into Dirk's chest. "I gotta man's job to do. And don't you get in my way while I'm doin' it." He shoved Dirk back a step, causing him to jab his back painfully into the corner of a bleacher seat.

Brett lumbered back to the parked Zamboni, and with surprising grace for a land mammal of such girth, clambered up onto the high seat. He gave the signal to one of the engineering guys in the main booth, and a section of the rink wall slowly began to open. As it did, the lights dimmed and the music quieted. Dirk rolled his eyes. Brett knew someone in management, and was able to get his own special entrance. Those in the crowd who didn't know what was up sat and waited; those who did know started chanting, "Zam-bone—nee. Zam-bone-nee." Then Brett stepped on the gas and zoomed onto the ice as the spotlight followed him across the middle of the rink to the roar of recorded crowd music (the actual roar was, thought Dirk, depressingly loud enough, but Brett wanted more). Then the lights turned back on and Brett went about his business, beginning his rounds and leaving behind a shiny smooth surface that glistened like the trail of an unusually tidy slug.

Dirk watched the crowd: they were all focused on the Zamboni, some pointing, most just sitting and staring, the air laden with strange fascination. Jealousy singed at Dirk; Brett sat there, surrounded with an air of flatulent self-importance that was almost visible as he commanded the crowd's attention. No sudden movement for the bathrooms or the food court, and those for the first few seconds, who talked, whispered. Whispered!

Dirk shook his head and prepared to continue his tour of duty, lowering the dirigible and heading it back towards the other end of the arena. It passed above Brett, who looked up, pointed and began to leer at the crowd, holding his right hand in the thumbs down gesture. Dirk watched in disbelief as the crowd began to take it up, pointing and booing at the dirigible as it made its way across the airspace.

Suddenly Brett whipped the Zamboni around and sped towards the center of the rink, slamming on the brakes and causing it to slide sideways before coming to a stop.

I didn't know they could do that, thought Dirk.

Then Brett stood up and made a lowering motion with both hands, getting the crowd to quiet down.

What the hell's he doing? thought Dirk. He could see Olsen, the facility manager, standing outside his booth with his hands on his hips, also staring at Brett. This was obviously not part of the ice maintenance routine.

The Zamboni driver put his hands to his mouth, and started shouting, his bray just audible above the general din of the room, "Zamboni rules, blimpie's a fool," until the crowd joined in. As the chant began to echo throughout the arena, Brett hopped back into the Zamboni's seat, stomped on the gas and began racing around the edge of the area, urging the crowd on, getting each section to try to be louder than the last.

Dirk stood in the corner, his face beet red, his body burned through with humiliation. That asshole Brett, he thought, one of these days ....

But as Brett zoomed past the end where Dirk stood, he reached into a damp shirt pocket and retrieved a pickled egg, hurling the soft missile straight into Dirk's slightly pimpled forehead.

Its vinegary contents splattered over his face and clothes. The smell of briny egg, coated with the filth of Brett's pocket and limned with the slimy residue of Brett's perpetually filthy hands, permeated the air. The crowd roared and a few followed suit, chucking wadded up napkins, crumpled popcorn boxes, chewing gum, and one half-eaten hot dog that caught him in the small of the back and stung like hell.

Dirk was overcome with rage. As he snarled vengeance at Brett, full of dark wishes involving auto-intercourse, incest, and several forms of bestiality, an idea sparked in his head.

He held the dirigible's controls to his chest, flicked the speed control switch to "Override High" and directed the balloon into a steep descent towards Brett, who stood on his Zamboni, hands raised into fists, awash in the admiration of the crowd like a victorious gladiator. The Airshark Mark II stole down, battered by a flak of snack food, packaging and miscellaneous arena detritus.

Brett sat back down, guffawing and pumping his fists, and never saw the dirigible until its nose impacted the back of his head.

Although such a device is, of course, filled with helium and therefore relatively light, there must be enough helium to lift the dirigible's frame and undercarriage; in this case 23 pounds of frame, engine, battery, and a complement of coupons. When traveling at 15 to 20 miles an hour, such mass can have a tremendous impact should it strike one's head, causing said head, for example, to kerplunk into the steering wheel of the Zamboni one may happen to be driving. Which in turn can cause collapse of certain nasal cartilage, the onset of blood and no small amount of pain.

There was a series of sounds that immediately changed the atmosphere of the arena: the slight "thump" of the dirigible hitting Brett, the very distinct "whack" of Brett's nose on the worn black steering wheel, and long, trailing howl of fear and pain emitted by the large man on the Zamboni that was about to careen into the wall of the ice rink. The ensuing splintering of the plywood retaining wall hushed the room entirely.

The balloon had stopped on impact with Brett's head, rose ten feet, then continued forward at a mad pace. Dirk, stunned by his own actions, had momentarily forgotten about it and was only reminded by the screams of small children and their parents, who were scrambling out of the thing's flight path. The dirigible, its nose now covered with the stains of discarded ketchup packets and a wadded up piece of grease paper that stuck over the pig's winking eye, was rendered in appearance from that of a particularly empty-headed member of Porky's family to that of a violently insane pirate hog, grinning a bloody, one-eyed grin.

Dirk worked the controls of the balloon, sending it up and away just in time to narrowly avoid a boy on crutches, who despite all that was going on, appeared from Dirk's reckoning to be howling a bit out of proportion to recent events. Dirk looked back down at Brett, who was sitting in the Zamboni's seat, one hand rubbing the back of his head, the other holding his nose, glancing about in bewilderment. Suddenly he turned to Dirk, a black rage written on his face, and jammed the Zamboni into reverse, its wheels spinning on the ice, raising steam as it crawled backwards. Then a screech of metal as Brett slammed it into "Drive" and spun towards Dirk, its wheels still hissing as they fought to grip the hockey rink floor.

Dirk's first reaction was to seek the fastest means of escape, but then an idea occurred to him.

He slowly smiled and raised the dirigible's remote control box high in the air so Brett could see. The dirigible, which had been trundling in a circle above center rink, suddenly pitched directly towards the floor and lunged down, the loose end of the grease paper eyepatch flapping against the side of the balloon. Brett turned to see what Dirk was looking at and understood at once that the chase had fundamentally changed. Dirk stepped aside as Brett crashed through the rink endwall and headed straight for the loading ramp exit, looking behind him as the leering porcine face loomed ever closer.

The Zamboni shot through the narrow exit doors, scattering fans and arena staff, and squealed around the corner of the ground level hallway. Dirk guided the dirigible through the doorway easily enough, but it was not built for close-quarters urban assault and crashed into a Feral Moles memorabilia stand, sending hats, mugs, ornamental flags and logoed shot glasses flying. In the silence that followed, Dirk could hear the Zamboni rumbling down the hall, Brett evidently either having not noticed he was no longer pursued or simply taking no chances.

Dirk walked slowly back to the rink, stepping over pieces of the plywood wall, food, plastic cups and other spent objects as people stared open-mouthed, moving aside to let him pass. He sauntered to the center of the ice and stopped, raising his arms as if to embrace the fans. Somebody yelled, "his name's Dirk!" someone else yelled, "Dirk Zeppelin!" and then the crowd began to chant, a section here, a few aisles there, then the Feral Moles themselves, the refs, and then the whole building, shouting, screaming, "Dirk Zeppelin! Dirk Zeppelin! Dirk Zeppelin!"

Dirk took a long, low bow. As he slowly raised his head, he saw Kelly standing in an entranceway in the far corner, a slight smile on her face. He caught her eye and held it.

Lost in the Static

The day after I heard that Ray and Rachael had broken up, I stopped by his apartment to see if he was ok. He's my older brother, but for a long time I've been the one who looks out for him. I didn't expect him to be a total mess or anything, but still, they had been pretty tight.

I found him in the living room, sitting on the floor by the stereo staring into space. He was holding a pair of black headphones—the kind with the really big earpieces, like soup cans—in his lap. He saw me and grunted, then, "Dave, you ever heard of a radio station called 'Radio for the Land of the Heart?'"

"No."

"What?"

"No," with emphasis.

He sighed, put the headphones back on and hunched over the stereo, an old one that was top of the line twenty years ago, fiddling with the dial. I noticed a stack of empty beer cans next to him, a Leaning Tower of Genesee with some smaller administrative beer structures surrounding it.

"Heartland Radio?" I asked. I could see that we would ease into the topic of Rachael; no going there straight away.

"Radio for the Land of the Heart."

"Yeah, whatever. Why are you looking for it?"

"It's ... it's just a great station. Gotta find it."

"What's so great about it?" I hoped I kept the annoyance out of my voice. Ray was quick to take offense, even with me. But I wanted to know if he was ok; we could listen to the radio later.

Except for the time he spent with Rachael, his job was pretty much his life. He had been working for a local contractor as a carpenter for the past ten years; he was kept on, despite his temper, because he was so good. Even if a project was finished and they had moved on to the next, Ray would come back after work to get a cabinet just right; maybe a door wasn't fitted to his satisfaction or the kitchen molding was a little off. Whatever it was, he'd work for free and keep at it 'til it was perfect. We both live in the same small town, Delhi, New York, and he had a reputation as a good worker, temper or no. So even if people avoided him socially, he was still considered a good man to have on the job.

He sat back, lifted the 'phones off his head and took a long pull from his beer. "I heard it the first night with Rachael. I'd asked her out at the Great American Grocery, right there in line with three people behind me. I figured for sure she'd heard about me and would say no, but what the hell, right?" —this was a shock, since it was the first time I'd heard that Ray was aware that people thought anything about him—"But she said, 'sure.' We went to Pizza Hut, then to the movies, saw 'Fight Club.'"

"That didn't have a 'Land of the Heart' radio station in it."

"I know Dave, that was later. But we had such a great time, she was just ...." He paused and looked up at me, hands in front of him, palms up.

"Yeah," I said. In some ways we understood each other at a pretty basic level. He was the one who told me to marry Beth, "She's the one for you man, I never seen you so happy." And he said it like he was looking right into me and could see that she was It. He just knew.

"So on the way back, we went parking." He laughed, then took another swig. "Yeah, like a couple of goddamn kids, about a mile up Federal Hill Road. I pulled the car into some hayfield."

I was surprised again. About the only thing other than work that Ray gave a shit about was his car. It was a 1979 Buick Century, metallic red and big as a house. He bought it for $300, painted it, rebuilt the motor and added chrome wheels. He washed it regularly and fretted about parking it in public places for fear of someone scratching it. The thought of Ray driving that car in a field—he must have been smitten with lust.

"So, you know, we ...."

"Yeah," I said, grinning.

"Afterwards we hung out, just lying in the back seat. Radio playing, drank a few beers, burned one, you know. Rachael fell asleep against me and I finished the joint, was sort of zoning, and next thing I know the radio's playing all these great tunes, ones from back when I was a kid."

Well shoot, I thought to myself, he was just stoned and listening to some oldies station.

"And?"

"I listened for about half an hour, then it faded out."

"Faded out?"

"Yeah, just got all static and went away. I tried to get it back but Rachael woke up and had to get home."

"So let's hear it," and I nodded at the stereo.

"That's just fucking it; I can't find it. I don't remember where it was on the dial. Christ, I don't even know if it was AM or FM. It sounded a little too rough for FM, but I never have it on AM. I don't know; Rach and I were kickin' around in the front seat for a while, maybe it got switched."

"Yeah, maybe. Listen Ray, I'm just making sure you're, you know ... things are cool. Want to come over and have dinner with us? Danny and Little Ray have been asking about you. They want to wrestle." Before Rachael, he probably spent more time with my sons than anyone else; they had something together. Almost like the two of us when we were kids.

But he wasn't listening anymore. He had put the headphones back on and cracked another beer. I watched for a minute as he slowly ran the dial up and down the band, and then, "Bye Ray."

He didn't answer.

❊ ❊ ❊

I didn't talk to him for about two weeks after that. Danny, my youngest, got sick and Beth had some important project to finish at work, so I had to stay home for a few days. The following weekend I had to fix a leaky pipe in the basement, then some catching up to do on my job, then ... you know, all that stuff. The older

you get the faster time goes, and one day you suddenly realize this isn't just a saying from people older than you.

Then one night, about 3:30 am, the phone rang. It scared the hell out of me
and I picked it up, my heart thudding in my chest. I could feel Beth sitting up
behind me.

"Hello?"

"Hey man, it's me. You got a radio there?"

"What?"

"You got a radio there?"

"Ray?"

There was a silence, as both of us processed the state of mind of the other. He
started again, this time slowly.

"Is-there-a-radio-there?"

"Ray, what is—" But I realized that this needed to be continued somewhere
else. I turned around and addressed the figure in the darkness—"It's ok, it's just
Ray. I think he's been drinking."

Beth settled back under the covers with an annoyed sigh and I took the cord-
less phone downstairs, out to the front porch.

"Ray, what's going on? Where are you? Is everything ok? Have you been—"

"DAVE! Just get to a radio! Please!"

That scared me more than the phone ringing, the pleading tone in his voice.
Never in my life did I imagine I'd hear my brother beg for anything, and sure as
fucking hell not with that sound in his voice.

I ran into the kitchen where we had one of those clock-radios screwed underneath a cabinet.

"Ok, Ray, I'm at a radio."

"Turn it on, AM, 1320."

I did, but all I got was static. "Ray, there's nothing but noise."

"Listen carefully."

I leaned my head close to the radio, my ear almost touching the speaker. The
hiss was punctuated only by sharp crackles and pops. Then, just for a moment,
something came through, barely. I think I heard music. It was possible anyway.

"I'm not sure Ray, maybe something for a second there, but—"

"You don't hear it?"

"Hear what?"

He mumbled something, then, "Try this." Suddenly a blast of white noise
made me pull the phone away from my ear. It lasted for about ten seconds, then,
"Dave, you hear it?"

40

"All I heard was static. What's going on?"

"I think I found it. I think Radio for the Land of the Heart is at AM 1320."

"Ok." I had that neutral tone just perfect.

"Yeah, I know there's some noise, but if you listen real careful, you can hear the tune. I think that was 'Dancing in the Moonlight.' Man, I love that song."

"Ray."

"Um?"

"Ray, you ok? Have you been drinking?"

"No, I just thought I found the goddamn radio station Dave. I thought fucking maybe you'd want to hear it."

"Ray, I just—"

"Fuck you, bro, when I find it I won't tell you. Then it'll be your tough shit."

✾ ✾ ✾

It happened at least four more times over the next couple of weeks; Ray would call and say that he had found the station, put the phone up to his stereo speaker and explain what song could be teased out of the hiss. I never actually heard any of it, but he believed he heard something. It didn't matter though. Sooner or later, whether by finally hearing the station identification or realizing that it was just noise, Ray would conclude that it wasn't "Land of the Heart" radio and try again.

He must have been trying a little too hard. I was in the grocery store one night after work, buying some ketchup so the boys wouldn't set up a howl at dinner. Bottle of Heinz in hand, I was walking towards the checkout when I ran into Ray's boss, Sandy.

"Hey Sandy, what's up?"

He was holding two large bags full of groceries and heading for the door, but when he saw me he stopped, put the bags on a nearby bench and turned to me with a serious look.

"Dave, you've got to talk to your brother."

"Hmm?" I've heard this before. Many times, actually. Usually the person I'm talking to goes on to tell me how they saw Ray the night before at the Mirkwood Inn or Dell's or some other bar, how Ray started out in a good mood, "but he was just throwing back those drinks, shots, beer, Christ Dave, he can down 'em," or something to that effect. I just nod and let them get on with it. Then they follow up with, "all of the sudden he got mad." Then the story devolves into how Ray, "went right after me Dave, and all I said was that he spilled something on my shirt," or "he tried to take on the whole bar Dave, I swear he wanted to fight

41

five guys, and they weren't small guys, either ..." sort of thing. No one is mad at me, not usually. All the locals understand that I have no control over him, but they always fill me in on the latest.

But this time it wasn't anything like that. Sandy just said, "Ray hasn't shown up for work in two weeks. 'Cept to pick up his check, last Thursday."

"Shoot Sandy, I don't know what's going on. I haven't seen him in a while; Beth and I have been real busy lately and—"

"I was there when he came into the office to get his check, Dave. He looked like hell. Pale, skinnier than usual, hadn't taken a shower in awhile." Sandy glanced around, then took a step closer. "I think you need to get him some help. Rehab maybe. He's on something."

I looked out the window.

"I haven't fired him yet. I can't do that; he's a fuc—He's a character, Dave, but I like the guy. He's one of the best I got." Sandy put his hand on my shoulder. "Listen, you get him in a program somewhere and you let me know. I'll do what I can to help you out. Your brother's a good man, we need him around."

I don't know if I ever heard anyone say that before. The measure of Sandy's decency wasn't just what he said, but also the fact that he walked away, pretending to check his watch while I pretended to scratch something around my eye.

Dinner was waiting, but instead of heading home I drove over to Ray's apartment. Walking up the staircase, I remember this particular feeling of dread, one that I always associate with Ray. It's hard to explain, but for years now, late at night or sometimes when I am focused on a job or fixing something in the basement, suddenly Ray will pop into my head and I'll be worried about him. No particular reason, but it's like there's this hole in my heart, waiting to be lined with a pain I've yet to discover. And it's got something to do with Ray. I'll feel bad, for him and for me. Like I have just an inkling of his sorrow, and there's nothing I can do about it.

He was inside. The place wasn't clean, but it wasn't any worse by Ray standards. He was lying on the couch, face pale, dark circles under his eyes. But I wasn't thinking drugs or drinking. I mean, he's my brother, and I could always tell when the guy wasn't straight. Although I wasn't exactly relieved either: it was clear that he hadn't slept for Lord knows how long. A long while. But before I could ask him what was going on with Sandy, he launched right into it.

"Dave, listen, did you know that radio waves can bounce off the atmosphere? Especially the AM waves; they can travel halfway across the country if conditions are right."

"Huh. Anyway, how are you feeling? You look a little tired."

"So I'm thinking that 'Land of the Heart' radio is coming from the Midwest. Makes sense, y'know? 'Heartland' and all that. I'm only getting it late at night when the conditions are right."

He saw the look on my face.

"It's not me Dave, it's true, there's lots of AM stations you can only get at night. Listen."

He got up and walked over to the stereo. It was already on and he turned up the volume, the speakers discharging a now-familiar scraping noise.

"It's just crap now, but around midnight, one o'clock, that's a classical music station out of Binghamton. That must be what, fifty, seventy miles from here? And this—"a twist of the dial, more of the same noise—"this is a heavy metal station, I'm pretty sure it's from Philly. You gotta wait until at least two a.m. to hear it. Heavy metal on AM radio. That's weird."

"Right. Ray, I ran into Sandy today and—"

"Yeah, yeah, where have I been." He turned the stereo off. "I got some vacation time coming. He'll just charge it against that."

"Yeah, but Ray, why?"

"Why what?"

"Why aren't you working?"

He looked at me as if I'd asked him whether he considered breathing important to daily living.

"You wouldn't get it." He turned back to the stereo, switching it back on and peering intently at the dial.

"C'mon Ray—what's going on?"

"I have to find that station. I know it's taking a lot of time but I only need a few more days. I've been keeping this chart—"He reached behind the stereo and pulled out a pad of lined yellow paper, thick with blue ink, a handmade grid covering the entire page and tiny handwriting filling each block—"I've been pretty methodical about it. I'm keeping this chart so I don't keep finding the same stations. Whenever I get something I listen to it for a while, make sure that's not it, then move on to the next one. I'm keeping track of both AM and FM."

"All that just to find a radio station? You just go up and down the dial, right?"

"It's not that easy. At night you might get two different stations on the same spot, depending on the time. 'Specially on AM. They fade in and out, so you have to keep the dial in one place for hours just to be sure. Like here, 590?" He turned and pointed at the stereo, near the lower end of the band. "Last night I got two different stations. WBZX during the day, plays oldies. They sign off at midnight, then I get this country station out of Wilkes-Barre. Around four in the morning WBZX starts up again."

Well, I thought to myself, that explained the lack of sleep.

"Hey," and he suddenly turned to me, "I've been meaning to ask—can you check the internet? The fucker might be on there, right? Most stations are. Look for—"

"—Radio for the Land of the Heart. Got it. Will do."

"Thanks, Dave," and I saw a smile crack his face. It was a little scary, like he was trying to be gracious. Ray did not have a computer and didn't give a damn about the internet. Ray was not gracious. Things were getting strange, and I should have had a clue right then and there what was coming.

"This is taking longer than I thought, you know?" he continued, scratching the stubble on his jaw and looking again at his chart. "'Course, as soon as I find that station ...."

I waited for him to finish the sentence, but he just stared down at the chart. After a few moments of silence I said goodbye and walked out, split between relief and worry. Relief, because Ray wasn't doing drugs or drinking (I mean Drinking; everything is relative). He was going through the standard girlfriend crisis, I told myself, just trying to deal with Rachael leaving. Maybe he thought the station would bring back memories or something. But eventually he'd find the station, nothing would happen, and he'd get over it.

Probably. That was the worry part.

So I tried to help; after dinner I spent an hour online, looking for "Radio for the Land of the Heart," "radio 1320," "radio 590," and so on. I tried every combination I could think of, but no luck. No radio station, anyway. "Land of the Heart" got me hundreds of hits, including a Mother's Day site, three travel agencies, a fantasy novel and several evangelical links. But no radio station.

That night, in bed, I told Beth about it. She said that we should spend more time with him, "invite him over for dinner, see if he wants to spend the night." That's when I knew it sounded bad to her too, because she never offered to have him stay over. Whenever he'd visit and dinner was through or when the movie ended, she'd wish him a good night and a safe walk home, the hint clear, regardless of the weather or late hour.

I went over to his place the next day after work. He was sleeping on the living room floor, headphones on and emanating a faint hiss. I shook him awake, waited for him to stagger back from the bathroom, and asked him over for dinner.

"Nah, I got to keep looking," he said, jerking his elbow towards the stereo.

The whole radio thing was getting to be a bit much, so I figured it was as good a time as any to bring up the other subject. "Seen Rachael lately?"

"She called me the other day. Wanted to go out."

I waited as Ray began picking up the empty beer cans and food wrappers scattered throughout the room.

"And?"

He went into the kitchen, his arms full of greasy paper and dripping aluminum. I heard the muffled crunch of the mess getting wedged into his overflowing wastebasket, and he walked back into the room.

"And what? I said no. It wasn't working out. She's nice, but ... I dunno. Kept trying to tell me what to do."

"But I thought you really like her. I mean—"

"—I do, Dave. We're still friends. I'm going to meet her for coffee the day after tomorrow."

"Then I don't get it. Why is it you want to find that radio station? I mean, I thought it had something to do with Rachael, getting her back, that sort of thing."

"Well shit, even if I wanted her back, what does the radio station have to do with it?"

"Well Christ, what is it about the station then? You're way too into this, Ray. I'm getting, you know, kinda worried."

He grimaced and turned his back to me, looking out the window at the streetlight illuminating the empty Main Street. "I don't know if I can explain it, Dave. There's just something about it, those songs the DJ was playing. It brought it all back. Like when I was a kid; those summers I used to hang out at Jim Coffey's house. We'd sit around on his front porch and watch the cars go by, just shooting the breeze. He'd play his brother's records and we'd spend all afternoon there; me, Jim, Ed Leno and Janice Strickland. Remember her? I had such a crush on her. Damn. Those were the days, man. Before things got all ... you know. I know I've—it was like the good times coming back over the radio." He nodded to himself. "Yeah."

Ray was silent for a moment; I thought he'd forgotten about me and was about to clear my throat when he continued:

"It's not that big a deal, really. I just want to listen to that station, see if they play more songs from those days. Get that feeling back. Maybe I can figure out how I'm going to ..." He shook his head then turned back around to face me. "Want a beer?"

I wish I had gotten him to finish that sentence. I don't know what he was going to say, but still I think it might have helped me find a way to reach in and bring him back from wherever he'd gone for the past decade or so. But I just let it go.

"No thanks. When are you going back to work?"

45

"Next Monday. I spoke to Sandy this afternoon, everything is cool. He needs me back and Sandy's a good guy anyway."

Walking out the door, I told myself that maybe the whole Rachael episode was good for Ray. "I am going to meet her for coffee," and "Sandy's a good guy," were just the sort of nice, well-adjusted things we'd all been hoping for years that he would start saying. When I told Beth, she said, "Maybe Ray's starting to figure out his priorities. Maybe he just needs a friend right now, he said he still got along with Rachael. He's a good man, Dave, he just needs to settle down and focus. Let's try again; invite him over sometime next week."

�֍ ✖ ✖

The next several days flew by with no word from him. I work for the county paper, a weekly, doing some graphic design, a little editing, a little sales, whatever needs to be done between me, three other employees and the owner. It pays well enough and I can lose myself in the job, trying to make the deadline and no mistakes, and everyone I work with is pretty calm under pressure. So I managed to forget about Ray, until one evening when Beth reminded me to invite him over.

Ray didn't answer the phone, but half the time he just ignores it so I figured I'd go ask in person. Pulling into his driveway, it took about two seconds to figure out he wasn't there. Car gone, lights out, mail piled up outside his door. I went back and told Beth.

"Maybe he's visiting some old friends. Maybe he went on vacation. After all Dave, it's not like he has to check in with you."

But she didn't believe any of it either.

The next night, 12:15 am, the phone rang. I felt a twinge of fear. Thinking of Ray and his car crumpled around a tree. Flames.

"Dave."

"Ray, man, where are you?"

"Missouri; just a few miles north of Joplin. Rt. 71 I think."

"Jesus Christ Ray, what the fuck are you doing in Missouri?" I could feel Beth sitting up behind me. "Missouri?" I heard her ask.

"Still trying to find Radio for the Land of the Heart, Dave."

Then I noticed how tired he sounded. And something else too, not quite like he was drunk, but there was an odd quality to his voice, a strain.

"Ray, listen to me, why don't you get to a motel and sit tight. I can—" I had to think; driving would take a couple of days, no way he'd be able to sit still for that long. We'd just about paid the credit cards off, but this was serious—"I'll get a plane to Joplin or wherever, and get you. We'll fly back together, I got it covered—"

"Dave, I don't need anyone to come and get me. That station's got to be around here somewhere."

"Ray—" I whispered through clenched teeth, "you got to—"

"Ahh shit Dave," his voice got tight, like he was starting to cry, "I been look-ing around for a week now, and I just can' find it. It's got to be here somewhere. Got to be."

"Ray, why didn't you tell me you were going to take off and go looking for it?"

"What the fuck were you gonna do? You think I'm crazy like everyone else. Screw you all. I have to find that station. I figured if I drove out here, look in person, I'd find it. I mean it reached all the way to goddamn Delhi, Dave. It's got to be some huge station. I haven't heard it but I will. And when I do, I'm going to find that DJ, sit in the booth with him and drink a beer and listen to the old days."

"Ray, please—"

A mechanical voice interrupted, informing us that Ray had to add two dollars within the next thirty seconds.

"Ray, listen, you got to stay where you are. I'll help you find the station, I'll—"

"Thanks Dave." He sounded different now, like he suddenly cheered up. "I'll be alright. I got some cash saved up, it's not like I been living high on the hog, know what I mean?" He laughed, a little too hard.

"Ray, please, man, please—"

"Twenty seconds," said the voice.

"Ray, call me back, collect."

"OK, I'll talk to you later."

I sat there for about half an hour, waiting for him to call. Eventually Beth said, "I don't think he's calling back David," and she gave me a hug. "Can you sleep? Want me to get you anything?"

I couldn't sleep and she couldn't get me anything, so I went downstairs and turned on the TV. There was nothing on so I walked out on the front porch and sat on the couch. It was one of those hot, humid summer nights, the kind where you'd better have air-conditioning or little need for sleep. We had AC in our bed-room as did the kids, but the rest of the place was a sauna. I got up and walked back into the house, crept upstairs and grabbed my jeans and a t-shirt. On my way out, Beth asked, "where are you going?"

"For a walk."

"Don't do anything ... silly, Dave. Please."

"Don't worry."

I stopped at the top of the stairs to open the door and peek into the boys' room. Danny and Little Ray were sound asleep. Danny was clutching a plastic fire truck; Ray was sprawled on the floor, his sheet wrapped around his body and neck. I unwrapped the sheet and put him back in bed. I gave them both a kiss, went downstairs to put on my clothes and walked out.

The Mirkwood Inn was only two blocks away from the house. It was almost empty, just the bartender and a lone customer, watching a "Star Trek" rerun. I got a seat with a good view of the TV, ordered a cold one, then another, and by the time I left I had managed to make myself tired.

❈ ❈ ❈

I floated through the next day, worried and hung over, trying to figure out what to do. That night, tired as I was, I still couldn't sleep, wondering if I should call the police, maybe try to find some sort of help line that Ray could call, something, anything. When I finally dozed off, it wasn't for long; the phone rang around 4:30 am.

"Dave!" He sounded positively joyful.

"Where are you?"

"Um ... Guthrie, Oklahoma. I think. Least that's what the sign at the liquor store says. Listen, I got some time on a phone card, so we have a few minutes."

Oh Jesus, I thought, he's getting further away. "Ray, please, please listen to me. Why can't you just wait and let me come out there? I'll help you find that station."

"That's why I called, buddy! I found the fucker! Hold on!"

The phone clanked down and a moment later I heard the clack and groan of a car door opening, then a blast of static, a faint beat just noticeable. He grabbed the phone again. "You hear it? Hear it Dave? Dave?"

"Maybe something. It's kind of rough though."

"Wait a minute," he said, and the phone smacked down again, dangling I assumed, by the cord in some godforsaken phone booth in Guthrie, Oklahoma.

He must have adjusted the dial, because it got clearer. There was a DJ talking, listing the last few songs that had been played, all of them sounding vaguely familiar, although I couldn't specifically recall any of the tunes. Then he started playing "Waterloo Sunset," by the Kinks, a song I swear I haven't heard since I was a teenager.

And it hit me. Like the way I think it must have hit Ray: the music brought back these memories, not of anything in particular, but a collage of those days when we were kids and everyone listened to AM radio. Long hours on the road during a family vacation and the miles passing by. Man-made beaches on Adirondack lakes, the thin layer of sand giving way to dirt in two plastic shovelfuls. Small amusement parks, the worn-out rides creaking their burden to screams and laughter. Gas stations illuminated by neon lights. Sitting in a diner, the sun blinding me through a window, ordering pancakes. I saw myself playing kick-the-can out behind the school, Ray running ahead of me and laughing. Then I'm throwing snowballs at cars. Dusk in winter, the cold, and the stillness.

"Dave? What's going on? Is Ray alright?" Beth asked, jerking me out of my reverie.

"Yeah, hold on," and I held up a finger.

The song ended, and the static increased again. I could barely hear the DJ, could just make out him saying, "This is radio ... at ... 'teen twenty, the music for the ... of the Heart."

Ray was right.

"See? See?" Ray demanded. "It's around here somewhere, it's gotta be. I'm close Dave, might take me a day or two, but I'll track it down."

"Ray, that station could be anywhere. You heard it from here, remember?"

"Yeah, right. Still. I must be getting close. Listen, I got to go. Station's fading, I got to drive around 'til it picks up again. Hang in there kid, say hi to Beth and the boys, and I'll call you from the station." He laughed, then, "Hey, maybe I'll get the DJ to dedicate a song to you. How about "Kung Fu Fighting? You used to dance around to that song, it was a riot. You were so serious."

"Ray, I can be there in—"

"Ok, little bro, gotta go. Later."

"Ray, wait!" I yelled as it hit me, the one thing he didn't say. "Where is it on the dial?"

But he hung up.

The next day I called the FCC—they never heard of it. I went back on the 'net and got the phone numbers for a bunch of radio stations in Oklahoma, called to ask them if they heard of the station. But I only got the same, "Radio what?"

I called stations in surrounding states, places selected at random, stations in cities and college towns in Kansas, Arkansas, Texas. No luck. But the Midwest is huge, right? I couldn't call every city, every town; I couldn't cover them all. It could be some desolate, on-the-edge-of-nowhere plains radio, their "Best of the '70's" hour-long special every third Tuesday of the month, and how would I find it?

A friend told me about pirate radio—guys who will set up their own small-wattage station out of their garage. Told me about these operations that set up on boats sailing up and down the Mississippi, trying to keep one step ahead of the FCC. But he doubted any pirate radio in the Midwest, even under the best conditions, would get as far as New York. But who knows? Ray definitely found something.

✣ ✣ ✣

That was all about three weeks ago. I haven't heard from him since.

I stayed up every night since that last phone call, crouched by the radio in the living room, trying to find the station. I went to Ray's apartment to get his chart, so I could pick up where he left off, but he must have taken it with him.

Last week I started staying home; I needed to catch up on my sleep. Beth didn't say anything, even though I was burning up vacation time that we had planned to use on a trip to the Finger Lakes. I could tell she was getting worried about me, though.

A few days ago I bought a bunch of maps of the Midwest, trying to figure out where Ray had been, where he might be going. He was methodical by nature; he must have some system for driving around and looking, listening. I was just guessing of course, but I had some ideas on how he might do it; he's my brother after all.

It was Beth's folks, Bud and Stacy, who got the show on the road, so to speak. Three days ago they stopped by for dinner and offered me money, "to help you find him," Stacy said. "To be honest, David, I don't know if I approve of him, but family is family."

I thanked Bud as he handed over a wad of cash, and I knew they were thinking it would go to a private detective, but I also knew there was only one way to do this.

The next morning, after Beth left with the boys for school and work, I took off.

✣ ✣ ✣

So here I am—driving north on the Interstate, heading out of Oklahoma into Kansas. My right arm is sore from holding it out and turning the radio dial all day.

Guthrie consisted of a post office, about a dozen homes, a general store, a diner and a liquor store. It took all of five minutes to learn from a waitress at the diner that Ray had been there (it's that small; they remember the strangers). He had left the same night he called me, after asking for directions to I-35.

I think I know what Ray was trying to find. It's like the rapid, scurrying movement at twilight that you see out of the corner of your eye when you're a kid. You turn to chase it and it's gone—but you know something was there. You stop

50

seeing it when things like girls, the price of gas, new appliances, become important. Or maybe you make yourself stop seeing it. But I remember, back then,
thinking that if I could only follow that thing, it would lead me to some secret
passageway, a hidden door at the back of my parents' closet or the entrance to a
small cave, covered by a bush out behind the barn. And if you could get through
the door or inside the cave, you'd find ... I don't know. Another world, I guess;
like those stories your folks read to you when you were little and they seemed as
real as anything else. Back then I could just feel it out there, lurking at the edge of
perception. Listening to that station, I got that feeling again, only stronger, like it
crawled out of that cave and grabbed me by the throat.

I have a plan. I know the station exists, and Ray's right, it is probably in the
Midwest. And he knows it exists, of course, and like the saying goes, he might be
crazy but he's not stupid. He'll find it eventually and he'll drink that beer with
the DJ. You could just tell by the DJ's voice that he was the kind of guy who'd let
visitors hang out.

So if I find that station, I find my brother. If I find it first, I'll just wait for
him. The kids can come out with their mother and stay with me until he shows
up. Either way, I'll get him, take him home, and make him better. Or try to,
anyway.

The exit is coming up, just a few miles to go and I'm in Wichita. The teenage
cashier at the last gas station told me there was a public radio station there that
plays "really old stuff."

Turning Dust

Nick sat on the couch, hot coffee and cigarette in hand to help cut through the haze of a new day. He was tired, having gotten up several times the night before to help Janice. He did that a lot now and the fatigue was beginning to feel normal, like ragged clothes worn every day; a shambling comfort amidst steady decay.

He was staring at a space two feet above the light blue shag carpeting as the morning sun shone through the opposite window, illuminating a gently swirling column of dust. Nick was absorbed in the languid motion of the particles, their varying size and shape just distinguishable in slow, scavenger flight.

The house was completely quiet. No creaking, no appliances ticking, humming, or buzzing, no planes overhead, no traffic outside, no TV, no radio. No Janice. Most importantly, no Janice.

The silence. It was, he thought, like looking at one of those notebook drawings of a three dimensional rectangle set at a slight angle—depending on your perspective, you were either looking down on it or up at it from below. The silence was like that too—it was either a roar or itself.

When he thought about it from the silence-as-silence perspective, the dust motes almost seemed to be moving in rhythm. That was what had so captured his attention: how could anything move in rhythm to silence? There was a connection there, but he couldn't quite get it; like seeing a face and having the name at the edge of cognition, ready to tip off if you could only give it a mental nudge.

The doorbell rang, interrupting his meditation. Nick shuffled over to the front door, his bare feet padding softly as he glanced down at his gray "Rolling Stones" sweatshirt and faded jeans. No stains, and his general presentation seemed ok for a Saturday morning. He wasn't expecting anyone, but her friends showed up all the time now. Not that his appearance mattered of course, but he often felt he was being judged by them and, to his annoyance, he cared.

Nick swung open the door and saw Henry standing before him, dressed in his usual sports-casual attire, Saturday or no—a navy sport coat over a blue oxford, khakis, battered running shoes (what Nick figured to be a nod towards a weekend state-of-mind) and the tweed hat that Henry always wore this time of year, its color a perfect match for his graying hair.

Henry's face, which Nick had once described as "strikingly bland," was finely etched with lines at the corners of his mouth and eyes. They were the same age, but Nick had so far escaped the more obvious signs. As for Henry, the small amount of forehead visible just under the brim of his hat bore creases as well, as if chiseled by a glacial burden, or, Nick thought with a familiar tightening of the stomach, the long rake of intense, well-deserved anger. Nick didn't like to think of himself as the sculptor, but he knew he tapped at least a few of those lines into place, regardless of more recent developments.

"Hello Henry."

"She here?"

"Yes."

He looked past Nick into the apartment.

"Where?"

"Upstairs."

Henry stared until Nick stepped back to let him in, their shoulders brushing as Henry passed and began climbing the stairs just beyond the doorway. It was strange; circumstances aside, Henry ought to ask permission to enter, much less go upstairs. But somehow Nick felt like the stranger in the house, careful not to offend his host's sensibilities. Nick knew Janice had met Henry at the coffee shop down the road—neutral territory—right after she found out, maybe a couple of times after that, but this was Henry's first visit here. Not that it wasn't appropriate, of course, Nick could hardly say no under the circumstances.

Nick watched as Henry tread slowly up the stairs, his head upright, never wavering, no glances to the right to view the photos on the wall, no looking to the left to survey the household domain from on high. Straight and true he ascended to the top, turned left and disappeared, no doubt walking down the short hallway to the bedroom.

Nick went back to the couch and sat down, reaching for his coffee. The smoke from the cigarette smoldering in the ashtray had joined the dust, adding texture to the image. He felt he was on the verge of something again and tried to concentrate, but he was too tired.

It had been a long night, even the OxyContin—dispensed to Nick by the pharmacist every two weeks, with grave warnings (or perhaps suggestions?) about the consequences of overdose—hadn't managed to quell the pain that radiated through Janice's body. The hospice people came by every day and offered to take shifts through the night too, but Nick insisted that the burden remain his alone, at least until sunrise. He didn't know why; except that perhaps he drew a mild comfort from the sacrifice, such as it was, on his part.

The pain—Nick thought of it as a thing, an awful thing in and of itself, and to himself he referred to it as "the Demon." He had knighted it as such in a moment of dark humor as he watched her writhe through a particularly bad evening, the gnawing in her bones causing her to moan and occasionally cry out. Of late he caught himself wondering if she actually was possessed, not quite comprehending how a simple biological process, out-of-control as it may be, could reduce someone to a gibbering husk begging for oblivion.

It had been five months since they got the news and she began her increasingly steep descent, this sum total of time flying by with pain-soaked ease. But the individual evenings, especially recently, seemed to have inverted the flow of time itself—they became entire days of pain in and of themselves, each minute stretched for maximum infliction of distress.

Lately he'd been feeling frozen, cracking his mold only to get to the office three or four days a week to sign a few documents, make some phone calls and delete 500 or so email messages (some read, most not). But mainly he just stared at his desk. They were good about it at work, his boss told him to do what he could and not worry about it, but that wouldn't last forever. Nick couldn't find the strength to care. He hadn't seen his children in weeks even though, despite her anger, Angie had been pretty good about letting them have weekend visits. He wasn't sure how much they minded his absence; the boys—eight and twelve—came when asked and dutifully followed him to museums, amusement parks and movies, but always with an air of numbed bewilderment that he was only too familiar with. Their relief upon being dropped back off at their mother's was almost tangible, as was his.

The sound of the bed creaking made him look up, and he wondered if he should go upstairs, his presence necessary because… No, he thought, not now. Especially not now.

✖ ✖ ✖

Nick had met Janice through a mutual friend, Roger. Roger and Nick headed their respective departments—Process Management and Finance—at an automotive parts manufacturer (muffler clamps—a conversation-killer every time the question was asked). Nick and Angie were regulars at Roger's bi-monthly parties; cookouts by the pool in the summer, cocktails by the fire in the winter.

Henry and Janice had first shown up at Roger's a year and a half earlier, invited by Roger's wife when they moved into a house just down the street. Nick gravitated towards Janice from the moment he saw her: he and Angie had been there for an hour, a nice buzz had just settled in, and then the front door opened and she had entered the house a few steps ahead of Henry. Nick was 30 feet away, standing in the doorway to the kitchen, when he looked across the room and caught her eyes. Later, when he tried to figure out exactly what it was about her, he thought maybe that's what it was, her eyes. Simple as it sounded, he felt there was some meaning in the intense blue that pulled him in when she was near; he couldn't look anywhere else or think of anything else but her. Those eyes.

They had stared at each other for a split second then both looked away, but there was that flash and he felt the energy, a metabolic boost from her physical presence, and he almost instinctively moved towards her without any idea of what he was about to do.

What he did do was introduce himself in a manner that Janice alone seemed to think charming; offering her a piggyback ride to Roger's homemade bar for a drink. To his surprise and delight she seemed inclined to take him up on it, but Henry's obviously forced smile brought them both back to reality. They chatted for a few minutes until Janice was obliged to circulate around the room with her husband. But throughout the night they kept re-engaging in a running conversation that excluded all others—she had picked up on a Dr. Who reference he had made, and they traded snatches of episodes—and each time he felt the spark, its brightness corresponding to her proximity and attention.

By the end of the night they were alone in the kitchen, deep in discussion about whether the Donner party used salt. She had disagreed with vigor; it was a ridiculous argument, they were obviously flirting and both knew it, but they kept it up until their respective spouses walked into the room. Whereupon said spouses, taking in the topic, the overly bright smiles, animated gestures and the general vibe, removed their mates from the room to go in separate directions, like parents escorting wayward children.

But they exchanged contact information, and two days later he contrived a question that he emailed her (he claimed to have forgotten the punch line to a bad joke she had told); they managed to agree that she needed to provide the answer in person. They met for a quick coffee that lasted two hours, and ended with a hug that lingered both the question and the answer.

Then it was lunch the next week—the unspoken agreement to go to a restaurant up the road in Troy, far from chance encounters with friends or colleagues. The hug again; perhaps a bit tighter, just a little longer.

Nothing followed though, not immediately. No lunches, phone calls or emails. As if they understood how close they were to something irrevocable, and wanting to take a breath, a chance to snap out of whatever joyful fugue was leading them out of their established lives.

The center held until Roger's next party. Nick seemed to have forgotten to tell Angie about the party until she made other plans, and then told her he'd be just stopping by for only an hour, tops.

Nick saw Janice when he arrived. Henry wasn't there, but he didn't bother to ask why. They tried to talk to other people at first, but those conversations got shorter, and the ones alone together in the kitchen, the hallway and back deck got longer, until they were drunkenly kissing under a tree in Roger's back yard. A shared cab home, and a show for the driver. From there it was a short journey to the more advanced forms of adultery.

After four months of furtive encounters, clichéd hotel engagements and back-seat romance, Janice moved out of Henry's house, Nick explained the new reality to Angie, and Janice and Nick rented a narrow townhouse apartment in downtown Albany, just a few blocks from the Capital building and several lives away from those they used to inhabit.

Compared to other marital re-alignments that Nick had observed, his was rather easy. Indeed, Nick convinced himself that despite his and Janice's seemingly successful efforts at discretion, deep down Henry and Angie simply must have known and thus, surprised reactions notwithstanding, tacitly approved. He had even convinced himself that someday Henry, upon being offered a presentation of the reasons why Nick and Janice were a perfect match, would see the obvious merits of the case and—grudgingly no doubt, which was understandable—concede the point. With grace even, if Nick had a few beers before he thought about it. Nick didn't go so far as to believe they'd be friends, but he would daydream of themselves as acquaintances who politely agreed to disagree.

On the other hand, he knew Angie too well to bother with such notions, and simply tried not to think about her. Once, a month after his departure, he tried to arrange a lunch, inviting her to a nice place downtown to discuss the kids, taxes and the remaining property issues—he wanted the T.V., had easily given up everything else, but didn't make a fuss over it at first for fear that she'd withhold it out of spite—but before he finished his proposition she interrupted with a laugh.

"Lunch? You're fucking kidding me, Nick. Feeling guilty? Want things to just be normal, whatever that is, between us? The kids will love us both, grow up happy and everyone neatly goes their separate ways?" He was silent, stunned by her scouring of his illusions. "Well, you can just forget it, cowboy. I'm hurt, I'm angry, and I got a gloriously vicious lawyer who'll go nuclear the minute I give the word. So you just keep up the child support—such as it is, for now—and stay the fuck away." And that was that.

As news of their new arrangement spread, Nick and Janice's circle of friends contracted so quickly he wondered if they'd been subjected to a malicious rumor; if instead of a simple change of pairings, someone had hinted at abuse, theft, or murder. It took Nick awhile to realize that unlike the relative balance of opinion with most of the divorces that he had seen, his and Janice's unexpected severances had resulted in almost universal sympathy for Henry and Angie, and the more negative spectrum of scorn to outright hostility for Nick and Janice.

For his part, Henry never issued any threats or even acted in a particularly intimidating manner. Except for the time when Nick, slightly drunk at a party they had all happened to attend (to the host's obvious embarrassment) a few months after the big split, tried to have a neutral chat with him.

Henry's face, the unremarkable facade then just beginning to acquire a layer of anger, swiftly transformed into that of a snarling dog—literally a dog; it struck Nick as absurd and he had to suppress a shocked giggle as he tried to remember the name of the breed—and Henry suggested that Nick never again attempt communication. Advice that Nick, shaken from his "acquaintances" theory, took to heart.

Janice came up to him minutes later, a smile on her face but when she got close she spoke through gritted teeth.

"I can't take it, Nick. No one will talk to me." She glanced around and hissed, "I mean, literally no one will speak to me. Let's just get out of here." Nick agreed. Along with the unpleasantness of Henry, he too found the room cold. Not as if no one would speak to him, but the small group with whom he usually engaged in conversation at gatherings like these, politics, the weather, luck of the Giants, seemed restrained. No jokes and neutral observations only—"yes, it has rained a lot lately."

Christ, I'm being shunned, Nick thought and shrugged. They would get over it someday. So he and Janice held hands as if preparing to jump in tandem off a bridge and made a completely unobstructed run for the door. He thought he'd heard one person say "Bye," and the sharpness of the tone managed to surprise him.

Thus detached, not only from their former spouses, but also from their entire social network—this was the last invitation they would receive for some time—they were forced to strike out on their own, and did so with abandon. Those first months together, Nick hadn't felt so full of unpredictable potential since he was a teenager. He discovered a passion for hiking, started going to the movies regularly, and Janice even got him back into tennis. They joined a Thursday night league and made new friends. Dinner out most nights, weekend trips to New York or Boston, the mountains. Sometimes they'd just sit in a bar and talk about all the things they had done or had yet to do. Money was tight for Nick; he was shocked to discover the costs of divorce—child support, attorney's fees, his share of credit card debt and car payments—but Janice made enough as a VP at an investment firm to cover the both of them with ease.

It was just before she got sick that he noticed it—a fading of events, as if the fabric of their relationship, their existence even, was beginning to wear thin and washed out, like winter light in the late afternoon. There were a couple of mornings, at the first instance of consciousness, where he found himself in a mild panic, as if he couldn't believe what he'd done, that it couldn't be real. Not that he wanted to take it back, but he wanted to call a time out and think about things some more. He had begun to wonder if all the running they were doing was designed to keep their minds off the specific sort of running they had already done. He was afraid that the energy, the lust intertwined with the excitement of new companionship was somehow false—a buzz that couldn't be sustained.

As for Janice, as far as he could tell she was—or had been—perfectly happy. She laughed with delight whenever he entered the room, kissed him every time she sat next to him, and flat out told him any number of times how happy she was. Nick knew she had spoken to Henry before she got sick, but it never bothered him. They had been high school sweethearts, together almost 20 years, and he wasn't so naïve to think that such a relationship would be so easily extinguished. In fact, their continued communication was one of the rationalizations he used to help justify his part in the modification of their relationship. It wasn't that bad, he'd tell himself, they remained friends after all. Even after the angry exchange over the telephone, he had tried again with Angie but she wasn't as ... sophisticated as Henry. He was left with only a vague sense of magnanimity; a veteran who's come to terms with the war, even if all the other side had not.

There were only two occasions when Nick noticed Janice seeming to be in any doubt. The first was a few days after they moved in together, a Friday night after they had been to the mall for dinner and a movie. They were lying side by side in bed, like they had been a couple forever. She was finishing up a book and he was about to turn off the TV, when he caught her looking out the window, the muscles on her jaw bunched with tension. She noticed his stare and smiled; it was forced, but he couldn't tell if it was for his sake or hers. Then she lay her head on his chest, jaws still clenched, put her arms around him and squeezed so tight he couldn't tell if she was trying to hang on or force him into a different shape; perhaps like the thing she saw out the window.

The other time was a few months later, the night Henry called and asked her to come back. Nick had just sat down on the couch next to her and could hear him talking, begging, saying he'd forgive her if she'd just come home. She put the phone down, crying, and gave Nick a wild look, almost accusing, then ran into the other room, saying it was "too late." Nick hung the phone up and smoked a cigarette, waiting to see what would come next. She came back in a few minutes, smiling, said not to worry and they went out to a bar. After a few gin and tonics he asked her about it; she said she didn't want to discuss it and they let it go at that.

✖ ✖ ✖

When the pain first started, she just said, "must be cramps," and shrugged. Nick went along, how could he know otherwise? When it didn't go away, he was mildly concerned, but she went to see her doctor mainly because they had planned a trip to Montreal and were afraid that some sort of minor ailment would jam up the plan.

Then came the chain of events that he'd heard about but never really paid attention to, along with a host of other bad things that didn't affect him directly. Tests, doctor visits filled with increasing somberness, dread, then the news, obvious before being verbalized. Therapy, poison actually, she tried to keep pace but was soon rendered to bed, the battle turning to a rout and the enemy lacking mercy.

Her friends returned. They had been trickling in since the rumor began circulating; when confirmed there came a flood of support.

Nick, though never made unwelcome, felt increasingly uncomfortable at the restored bond between Janice and the representatives of her Henry life. Everyone was quite friendly, but there was a scent of blame in the air, a sliver of judgment in the quick looks and faster smiles. Despite their close company in such circumstances, Nick didn't think any lasting relationships were being built between him and Janice's friends.

As for his own friends, a few started speaking to him again and a few more were pretty much done with him. He didn't mind the latter; what he did mind among the former was the sense of embarrassment about Janice, as if it was all a tragic mistake that their ridiculous fuck-up friend Nick had caused despite their best efforts to help him.

And there it was, he thought, a straightforward move—leave their respective spouses—that seemed to make sense at the time, but who knew? He just didn't understand his role anymore, and there were obligations he could sense but didn't know how to perform.

✖ ✖ ✖

He figured he should check on how Henry was doing. As he began to climb the stairs, he wondered why he felt like apologizing to the man.

Nick slowed as he turned the corner of the hallway and looked into the bedroom. The sun was shining in through the window and he could see the faint waves of dust motes gliding through the light. Part of him wanted to go back downstairs to compare patterns of motion.

But it was the bed that captured his attention. Henry, fully clothed, had gotten in with Janice. She lay in his arms, her head on his chest and he was whispering to her, Nick could barely make it out, "shh, just listen to my heartbeat, shh…." and gently rubbing her back. Henry glanced up when Nick stepped softly into the room, but returned his attention to Janice.

The fear—for days now he could feel it, smell it on her, and was ashamed that he'd never been able to lessen it—it was gone from the room. There was a look of peace on her face that not even the drugs had been able to bring, a stillness she possessed—a posture that Nick had always assumed Janice would acquire as their lives settled into each other's, but she never quite made it. It wasn't a relative calm either, not the pause of an otherwise agony-wracked soul slowly diminishing, but rather an absolute peace, one that he knew, if only by looking at her lying with

Henry, comes with a profound contentment. The word "complete" went through his mind, and he wondered what he had done, what damage his actions had wrought. She had attained a beautiful detachment in the presence of her match; found sanctuary as a sympathetic vibration, and he thought of the dust swirling to music he could not hear.

Jack and Diane

It was a late Tuesday morning and Slappy's Diner had emptied of the farmers, truckers, travelers, and bright-eyed, bushy-tailed, SUNY Morrisville students who had wandered in for breakfast: the eggs and bacon or sausage, the pancakes, or the "Slappy Special" (pancakes, eggs and bacon or sausage).

Sitting in a booth next to the window, Diane rested her chin in one hand while twirling her hair with the other, watching Jack upend a bottle of Frank's Red Hot sauce over his scrambled eggs. The sun was shining in through the windows that overlooked Rt. 20, adding a squint to her frown that grew with each thick drop of the bright red liquid onto the steaming yellow and white mass.

Jack pushed an errant lock of graying hair out of his face, oblivious to her stare. The sun made him squint too, and Diane looked at the lines extending from his eyes. He didn't quite look his age, she thought with a mixture of pride and

63

mild annoyance. All he'd been through and he still managed to convey a sense of youth, forty going on thirty-two. She hoped she was holding it together as well. She knew she was, but she had to work at it. Jack just ... was Jack.

Jesus, she thought as he kept shaking the bottle over his eggs, why don't you just pour gasoline on them, set them on fire, and shovel 'em down the hatch? God, his digestive tract must be one long series of scar tissue. She shook her head.

"Want some?" Jack asked, looking up as he pushed his black-framed glasses up his nose.

"No thanks, Babe," Diane said, smiling. Despite the years of her giving the same answer, he still always asked. But she appreciated the fact that he did, she knew it was a sincere offer. He just couldn't quite comprehend how she could not like hot sauce on her eggs, as if he was convinced that for the past two decades she had just forgotten that she liked it, and it was only a matter of time and repeatedly asking until she'd remember that indeed, she actually did like hot sauce on her eggs. By Golly.

The waitress approached. "More coffee, hon?"

"Thank you Miranda," Diane said, nodding.

Jack looked at her for a moment before shaking his head. "Jesus. You're going to burn a hole in your stomach." He turned to look up at the waitress. "Has she drank the whole pot yet? You're going to have to cut her off soon."

"Jack," Diane replied softly, "it keeps me going. You know that." She turned and dipped her head to hide one eye from Miranda and winked at him. For added emphasis, she extended her leg and rubbed her foot on his shin.

She saw the flicker in his eyes. They still had it, even after all these years, even in the wake of all the jobs and the moves, new friends, old friends and split friends. Even in the wake of Jack.

Why not, she thought. We've got nothing else going on today. An afternoon spent in bed, screwing, drinking coffee and watching movies with the shades pulled down would be just the thing. Defy the world, or at least their immediate circumstances.

Then a twinge, as she remembered the suitcase sitting in the back of the closet, underneath a pile of clothes. The one she'd packed the night before, while Jack was out for his evening walk. The one that she had been mentally packing since two weeks ago when he first told her the news, that his contract was up at the end of the Spring semester and the college had, somewhat predictably, decided not to renew it for the Fall semester.

"I'm sorry, babe," he had said, "I guess it's time to move again."

She knew it was time to move, oh she agreed with that all right, but the move she had in mind was from Jack, not with him. Not anymore.

Diane sighed as she stared out the window at their car, a ten year old Chevy Caprice. He could keep the car, she was going to take the Greyhound to Syracuse, then a flight to Boston. She had made arrangements to live with a friend, a woman with a rich, stable husband and an extra bedroom. Several bedrooms, in fact, and, she knew, a bathroom for each.

She noticed he was staring at her. "Zoning?" he asked.

"Just thinking," she said.

"Don't worry, we'll get by."

"Mmm," she replied. They had always gotten by. It was overrated. Jack's adjuncting never paid much, not as much as her bartending did, which meant that they always had to find the silver lining in the otherwise gray cloud of the working poor. No mortgage to worry about, true, and she made sure they never let the credit card—her credit card, Jack never had one—get them into trouble. They could always just manage food, rent, utilities, and enough extra cash to keep in motion whatever smoke-spewing pile of disagreeable auto parts they happened to own at any given time. Jack always managed to get the health insurance. Otherwise, they owned very little: some clothes, an old stereo, a virus-riddled pc, basic furniture and several boxes of Jack's books and music that Diane threatened to toss out every time they moved.

"My God Jack, the Carpenters?" she had asked during one of the moves when she opened the box, thinking it contained dishes. "When was the last time you listened to them? Did you ever listen to them? And if so, why?"

"They're cool babe. In a kitschy kind of way," he had replied.

But that album was in her suitcase now. On a whim, just before Jack got home, she pulled it out of the box. She thought that someday she'd listen to it and think of Jack.

She actually had gone and thrown out a crate of moldering science fiction paperbacks he'd had since they first met. She had never seen him read or even remove any from the milk crate he'd kept them in. Apartment ballast, he jokingly called them, but two moves ago she hid them under an old carpet they had left on the curb. He still hadn't noticed.

A young woman pulled up to the diner in front of their window and got out of the car. She opened the back door, leaned in and after a minute of fussing, backed out with a baby in her arms.

Watching them, Diane felt a tug. Something, loss or anger or both, she didn't know. She was leaving Jack, but not much else. A few possessions, a couple of friends. But no babies, no children.

The day, several years ago, after the tests: the doctor had asked, "Have you thought about adoption?"

She and Jack, sitting in the doctor's office and absorbing the news, nodded thoughtfully at the suggestion. Jack took the card from the agency that the doctor slid across his desk and pretended to read it.

But they never spoke about it, they didn't need to. Until Jack held down a steady job, at the very least, no one was ever going to let them adopt a child, and that was assuming—a big assumption—that they wouldn't discover why Jack had such trouble keeping a job in the past. And even if they somehow remained ignorant of that particular 800 pound gorilla swinging through the trees of his personal history, she doubted they could afford the whole deal anyway.

She had some money now, though, had stashed it in the suitcase. A lot of it, actually. Tips, skimmed paychecks, whatever she could save. Originally it was a slush fund for a trip to Paris, romance and the like, the wrinkled bills crammed into the case of a broken vacuum, a safe place where Jack would never look, not even back in the day when he'd feverishly scour the apartment for cash, change, the stereo or the TV. Well, not the whole stereo, he only sold the cassette player ("real rock is played on records, baby," he said later). They went through three TV sets. As for her jewelry, she forgave him for all but the claddagh ring her mother had given her a long time ago. Even now, the thought of that one generated a wisp of anger.

Eventually it became emergency money, for bail, the ER, or rehab, wherever Jack ended up first, but somehow it was never needed.

Then it became a way out.

She was confident she'd be able to start over again somewhere else. She'd been bartending for almost twenty years now. You could count on death, she thought, and taxes, and also that almost every town in the country has a bar that is looking for help. The tips were usually good and she could still draw the undivided attention of the boys (and a few girls).

It was getting old though, it had been old for a long time. She had gotten a degree in Business Communications, but never quite found regular work. At first, when Jack was in grad school, there seemed no need to hurry to a career, tending bar was fun and helped pay the rent. The plan was to wait for Jack to get his first teaching job, then look for real work in whatever town they settled in.

But it never quite materialized, and the career—whatever it was to be—receded into the distance; it wasn't even an active dream anymore. She was too old to start something new, something that would bring in real money, a bonus, a retirement plan or stock options. Free drinks and rancid popcorn were the extent of her fringes, she thought bitterly.

Got to keep my perspective, she thought. I'm doing something about all this. Maybe the high-end perks are gone, but it's not too late to hold out for a job with regular hours. Health insurance and working with people her own age. Discussions about the weather, the best vacation destinations, or how to handle a kitchen remodeling project.

For a moment, she pictured Jack holding a hammer, and almost laughed.

At 38, she was well-versed in the personal exploits of Lil' Wayne, could sing along with Carly Rae Jepsen's "Call Me Maybe," knew enough to be flattered when told, "you got the cake," and was slowly but steadily going deaf from the years of being subjected to music blasting out of sound systems of countless happy hour celebrations in countless college towns throughout New York.

And one of these days, some wisecracking college boy—there were so, so many of them—was going to get a pitcher full of whatever cheap squirrel-piss she was serving cracked over his stupid, leering head, so help her God.

She took a breath. No point getting worked up now.

Jack called out to the waitress, "Miranda, is the paper here?"

"Sure," Miranda said, and brought it over from a nearby table. Jack unfolded it, pulled out the last section and spread it out before him.

"Classifieds?" Diane asked.

"Why not?"

"Well, I don't think the colleges put ads in the paper—or at least that paper—for jobs, hon. Not your kind anyway."

Jack nodded. "Maybe it's time I looked for something else anyway."

Diane turned back to look out the window. A semi was crawling its way up the hill past the restaurant, backing up traffic behind it. "DLM, Ottawa, Ontario," was written in bright yellow letters on the side, and for a moment Diane felt the urge to run out and jump in the cab. Leave it all behind, even the suitcase and cash and whatever possessions she had bothered to pack, just beg the driver for a ride, hand him her credit card and tell him to keep it, just get her to Canada.

Jack said, "I know." Diane spun around to face him. He was staring at her, a mixture of sorrow and mild amusement on his face.

"I always say that," Jack continued, looking past her at the truck. "Sometimes, though...."

He's thinking the same thing, she thought. She lowered her eyes and felt a brief flare of hurt, then smiled at her own hypocrisy. There was only one packed suitcase in the apartment.

She doubted—no, she knew—that Jack would never think of leaving her. It just wasn't in him. Back then, at its worst, he'd get home late at night, out of his mind. He'd come straight to bed, hold her tight, his heart pounding and too much sweat for not much going on, but his head pressed to hers and he'd whisper, "I love you, I love you," over and over again. It was, she thought, the only positive thing about the coke. He didn't do that anymore.

The pen in his hand was poised over the newspaper, a circle drawn around a small ad. She glanced at his face; he was still looking out the window. She leaned forward to see what he had marked. "IT Manager," it said in bold letters.

He's losing his mind, she thought. Jack had only barely mastered the nuances of getting email. Sending it was a project for some other time.

Until he broke the news, she allowed herself to hope that this job might last for a while. Jack had been straight for two years and it was clear that he had finally attained some balance. She quickly scanned his face for signs of strain, but there was only the usual lost-in-the-moment-Jack, his attention focused on the immediate thing in front of him. She wondered how long it would take him to notice if she spontaneously combusted.

Morrisville had hired him as the result of probably the last favor from an old friend from downstate. Former best friend, actually, before some unpleasantness involving the friend's dog and Jack's propensity to drive too fast through residential neighborhoods. His friend's latest novel, a Pulitzer contender, had provided him the stature to call up Chairs of English Departments at other colleges and ask if they'd hire Jack, despite his reputation. Or, to Jack's credit, with what was left of it.

Jack had some promise at one time, that and money, due to a movie that was made based on a poem he'd written a few years out of grad school. He didn't really consider himself a poet and wrote only occasionally, but he'd hit the jackpot on this one, a moving account about a young man's struggle with LSD, and the poem's publication in the New Yorker inspired a screenwriter. Which in turn led to a film of some critical acclaim, and almost complete anonymity amongst audiences.

But in academic circles, his fame was complete, as the author of the only modern poem that had been converted to the most significant medium of the day. And which made said author a bucket load of money to boot, for a change.

That was the peak, she thought, remembering the parties, a few interviews, and the expectations that it was only the beginning. She'd packed two reviews of the movie and a photo of her and Jack standing with the film's star, a swimsuit model who actually was a very good actress despite the burden of her former profession. But the decline was gentle, steady, and as unstoppable as the tide. If, of course, the tide was composed of coca extract with traces of whiskey and vodka.

Diane shook her head, causing Jack to glance up from his review of the opportunities in the high tech field.

He had been hired as an assistant producer and although he had done little on the movie, he was paid very well. After its release, he had gotten a job as an assistant professor at Columbia, and kept getting invited to parties. Eventually he went to as many without her as with her, coming home too drunk, stoned, high or generally twisted to make much sense, even if he did seem to want to tell her everything he did that day. Twice.

Over time, classes were increasingly missed, slept through, forgotten or simply deemed less important than what he was snorting at the time. His fame ebbed, and after a few years, it was suggested that his genius might be needed elsewhere.

They worked their way upstate; another assistant professor position at Pace (two years; the last straw an unapproved, week long mid-semester "sabbatical" at some shithole in the Bronx where she finally found him and dragged him away from the threat of exactly one gun and two knives); Bard (two years; campus security had found him hunched over his desk with, literally, a straw up his nose. No charges if he left quickly and quietly); SUNY Albany, Case Western Reserve in Cleveland, SUNY Alfred, Colgate, SUNY Delhi (two, two, one, one, one; coke, coke, lingering effects of coke, bad luck, stupidity).

His recovery came about abruptly. There was no "incident" as such, not like with everyone else she'd heard or read about. No car accident, OD, incarceration, girlfriend or even a particular job firing that did it.

It was late summer, and Jack had finished teaching a summer course at St. Lawrence University, way up in northern New York. It didn't look like he'd get renewed for the fall semester. But they had some cash saved and lived under the reign of a sympathetic landlord, so they decided to stay put in the village until he found something else.

To this day, she didn't know what it was. He'd been out the night before with a grad student and some townies, got in late as he usually did, mumbled sweet ramblings in her ear, and passed out. She thought he said something like, "witches." The next morning, he just literally got out of bed, still smelling of sour whiskey, and said, "I've got to stop." She had doubted if he was straight at the very moment. He threw on some crusty jeans and a stained "Warren Zevon," t-shirt and walked out of the house, not to return until dinner.

Through September and October, he left the house every morning and spent the day walking along the county roads that led out of the village. "Walking and thinking," he told her the second day. That was all she got from him, but she didn't want to mess up his strange and abrupt recovery, so she stopped asking questions.

Jack more or less stayed straight ever since. And every day he still went for a walk, though rarely all day anymore.

It sounded therapeutic. In theory she thought it would be good for her too, but she never could seem to get the energy to walk with him. Not after a late night on the job. Maybe in her next life, the one that waited at the mouth of the open suitcase, she'd start walking. Start over, like Jack, and start walking. I'm walking now, she thought.

Even after he cleaned up, Jack's absentmindedness, or maybe it was just bad luck, at one time somewhat endearing, had caused him almost as much trouble as his nose.

SUNY Alfred. Sleeping through class. It wasn't fair, she thought. It had been the fall semester, right after he started to get clean. The college had hired him just before classes started and they left St. Lawrence to start over in western New York. Despite his exercise and the obvious improvement in his condition, his body was still adjusting to an untainted regimen. Among other things, he had trouble sleeping at night. But he could sleep just fine, it seemed, during the day.

Colgate. Diane shook her head as she gently rotated her coffee cup in her hands. She loved the village, Hamilton, a picturesque stereotype of a sleepy upstate college town. They lived in an apartment located in the back of a huge stone mansion on the main street. Every morning she'd get up and get coffee and a croissant at a nearby bakery. On warm days, she'd sit on a bench at a small park between the apartment and the bakery and watch traffic while she sipped the coffee. She didn't make many friends, but it seemed that everyone was generally nice.

She had thought about going back. But she wouldn't have a free place to stay while looking for work, and didn't dare burn up her savings on the hope that something would come along. Maybe if she was able to save more in Boston she'd try to go back.

Jack's termination wasn't entirely his fault. A fellow adjunct/abuser by the name of Pete Holmes went on a two-day bender and thought he'd swing by to pay Jack a visit. Jack decided he'd try and talk the guy out of his problem by convincing him to use the "walk in the woods" therapy.

Pete also happened to be a pilot who enjoyed flying with a good buzz on, and despite the obvious danger, Jack accompanied him to the local airfield (literally a field) and went up in the plane with him, thinking that it would be a good opportunity to get Pete to focus on what he was saying.

They ended up in Las Vegas, with no way home. It turned out that Pete could fly a plane just fine while drunk, but couldn't maneuver a rented Taurus out of a parking lot without hitting three parked cars and a security guard. Diane had just enough money to wire Jack bus fare; Pete's fate remained in the hands of the local constabulary. The trip back to Hamilton took three days, the same three days he was supposed to be giving finals, and the ruckus that ensued left Jack without an invitation to come back.

There were real lapses as well, of course, including one spectacular one when they were living in Cleveland. It was the weekend that The Who were inducted into the Rock 'n Roll Hall of Fame and Jack, after being given an unusually generous amount of Bolivia's finest from an admiring student, had filched Diane's credit card and bought a scooter. He then paid a ridiculous amount of money for a welder to attach a bunch of mirrors to the thing in honor of "Quadrophenia," and proceeded to drive to the Hall of Fame. Coked to the gills and singing selections from "Who's Next" and "Face Dances" at the top of his lungs, he was riding down the wrong side of the road at noon in downtown Cleveland when, according to what he later told police, he was suddenly "blinded by the sun reflecting off all those fucking mirrors," and ran into the back of a pickup truck that was overloaded with hay bales. It was widely assumed that the nature of such cargo accounted for his continued presence among the living and independently mobile. No hospital, no jail, although for a long time, no license.

By the time he got a job at SUNY Delhi, he had more or less stabilized. But his newfound acquaintance with reality required some getting used to, and Jack was unable to measure his perspective.

Hence the flag-burning incident. Jack, eager to do his part in the faculty's efforts to oppose some rumored staff cuts, decided to stage a one-man protest.

But Jack's limited PR skills were not up to the task, as the controversy he planned failed to materialize. In no small part because he hadn't bothered to tell anyone what he was doing, nor had he given any thought to the time and venue, conducting the demonstration at 7:45 am on a Monday morning in front of the administration building.

Despite the lack of any press, a crowd, or even a few disinterested strangers, Jack went through with it, unfolding the pillowcase-sized Old Glory he'd purchased from a Wal-Mart and lighting it up as he held it aloft with one hand and reading from notes that he held in the other hand.

He soon had lost his place in his prepared ramblings, yet still impressed himself enough to keep barreling ahead in an impassioned manner, having managed to work in Nathan Hale, Ronald Reagan (for irony's sake) and a wildly inaccurate account of the Mexican Revolution. His voice shaking with outrage, he waived the blazing flag around with increasing vigor until he realized that his sleeve was on fire.

With a yelp he tossed the flag to the ground. Said piece of ground being occupied by a cat that, up to that point, had been Jack's only sentient audience, but whose attention had drifted to a chipmunk in a nearby tree. The cat, not caring about Poncho Villa's attack on the Alamo and thus focused on the rodent, never saw the flaming colors until it was nearly too late.

It was at that moment that two half-awake freshmen decided to take a look out their dorm window and saw what was later termed, "a savage attack on a kitten." Since one of the freshmen was a new member of the local chapter of PETA, a fuss resulted.

Diane paused for a moment. Jack had lit the flag with the lighter he'd gotten her as a birthday present, back when she used to smoke. It was engraved, "I loved you even before I met you. Jack." It still meant a lot to her, but she realized now that she forgot to pack it.

She shook her head; it made her cry when he gave it to her, and even now, on the verge of this, it brought something back. She'd have to get it before she left.

The controversy that Jack had in fact managed to generate resulted in beer-fueled demonstrations outside the same administration office, only this time complete with crowds and press. In the end, he had to publicly apologize, and the college had to promise free medical care to any stray animals brought to its veterinary science center.

"Goddamn freaks," he later said of the students, "Animal rights? What about our imperialist foreign policy? The plight of the urban—hell, the rural too—poor? World hunger. Racism. Who," and he pointed a finger at Diane for emphasis, "gives a shit about cats? These kids, they have no perspective. They're to the militant left of Marx! Show me where in Das Kapital Marx wrote anything about how cats will play a role in the rev-o-fucking-lution!"

"Jack, please calm down," Diane pleaded from across the Faculty Chair's dinner table, where they were supposed to be enjoying the department's annual fall dinner. This was a week after things had quieted, but Jack, although free of any alcohol or drugs, had been drinking the Chair's imported espresso all night and was wired.

"For all I know," he continued, oblivious to the stares of his colleagues, "Marx himself was the one who figured out that you can ram an electrode up a weasel's ass to get an unspoiled pelt. Even the commies wanted good fur coats to stay warm."

It was shortly thereafter that the Dean, sensing an opportunity to tactically dispose of a loose cannon from the faculty deck, decided that perhaps the admin folks were right in that exactly one job cut was for the greater good. Jack and Diane were on the road again the next semester.

The lighter, Diane thought. It was either in her top dresser drawer, or in a small wooden box that sat on the bookshelf.

"What about Mexico?" Jack asked, startling her.

"What?"

"Mexico," he said. "Maybe I can find some expat school down there, teach English Lit to diplomats' kids."

"Sounds good to me," she answered, trying to keep the flatness out of her voice. Maybe he was kidding, maybe he wasn't, but she didn't want to talk about the future with him. Not now. Suddenly she felt an urge to cry and looked away.

"Yeah, Mexico," Jack mumbled, and out of the corner of her eye she saw he had returned to his perusal of the classifieds.

Last year, Jack had gotten the adjunct job here at Morrisville. Diane, determined not to let him repeat past mistakes, carefully monitored his activities throughout the semester, making it a point to ask about his day, his relationship to the faculty, his plans for the weekend.

He had done well. She attended a few parties with him, and it was clear he got along well with his fellow teachers. He stayed out of trouble, coming home after class, going for his walk and reading or preparing for the next day. On weekends they went for drives, attended plays by the school's drama department, went to basketball games (one of Jack's students was on the team), or occasionally drove to Syracuse for lunch.

The students liked him too. Every now and then she'd stop by his class and watch him teach. He still loved it, anyone could see, and now, thinking about how he looked when he was in front of a class, pacing back and forth, making jokes, drawing the students out of their shells, trying his best to bring them into his world, she felt it, whatever it was that had faded. The feeling was here now though, and although she knew it would fade again, she smiled, glancing at him and shaking her head. Jack. What am I going to do without you?

"Mr. DeLaney, yeah, the dude's all right," one student had told her last week after she asked him what he thought of Jack. She was bartending in "The Matador," the local college bar, and noticed that the kid was carrying Jack's required reading as he ordered a Long Island Iced Tea.

"I mean, some of this shit is pretty hard, and who cares anyway? But DeLaney will walk you through it, know what I mean? He's got a sense of humor too; he's a funny fucker." The kid paused as he scanned the room, presumably looking for fellow Long Island Iced Tea drinkers, then looked back at Diane. "That, and his classes don't necessarily start on time, so you got some slack. Sometimes he'll wind it up early, too." The kid glanced up from his careful study of Diane's breasts. "You his girlfriend?"

"Wife. That'll be five bucks," she said. The boy's eyes dived to her chest again. She glanced at a pitcher sitting on the counter below the bar and entertained a thought.

"Wow," he said, "He is definitely doing all right." The kid, skull intact, left a two dollar tip.

Jack's favorite class was creative writing. Among the techniques he used to coax stories out of the students was to designate a theme class once or twice a semester. Students would write a short story related to a stated topic or idea, then read and explain the story in class. Judging from the reaction of students at previous schools, Diane knew it was a popular exercise.

"It always gets 'em going," he had explained to Diane, describing the first theme, "All messed up."

"You get the standard stories of drinking, drugging and whoring, although some are pretty intense."

"Are any true?" He would know.

"Not many," Jack said. "Mainly regurgitated from movies. For most, anyway."

"Do you ... ever talk about it with the kids who don't make it up?"

He paused. "Nope. This isn't therapy, and there isn't anything useful we can tell each other."

Here at Morrisville, it was the second theme class that had done him in. By early April, Jack had complained that the kids, "weren't really trying anymore. I've got some good writers, but they just won't do it, make the effort and say it."

"What do you mean?" she asked.

"They won't open it up. Too much about how things ought to be or might be, not how things are."

"What about those drug stories?"

"They're all the same. Different drugs for different generations, I suppose, but the same experiences. Anyone can write about the times they were fucked up. I want 'em to write about the times they wished they were fucked up."

"So what are you going to do?" she asked.

"I have an idea," Jack said, nodding to himself. "I gotta get these guys to put their hearts into it."

"Well, good luck," she had said, and turned back to her magazine. She was looking at a cruise ship ad, a glossy photo of a gleaming white, stadium-sized ocean liner sedately sailing on an impossibly blue Caribbean sea.

Now she wished she had stopped dreaming and asked him what he had in mind to get the kids "hearts in it." She would have talked him out of it.

Jack announced the theme at the next class, "Baring Your Soul," and, significantly, said that he would participate as well. As Diane later learned from the giggling students who made their way to the Matador, Jack's expression of soul involved conducting his class in his usual attire of t-shirt, sport coat and scuffed dress boots. This time, however, sans trousers.

"Well, hell, Diane, I didn't come in any ridiculous tighty-whitey's, or some perverted crotch-hugging thing," he later sputtered in defense of his method, "they were a perfectly respectable pair of well-laundered, fully covering boxers. Nice plaid design. I thought it would keep the mood light, on a topic like this, these kids can get into heavy stuff, y'know?" He shook his head. "Christ, if it had been summer and we'd been on a golf course at some faculty outing, I would've been complimented on my taste in shorts. For all I know, the goddamned things have pockets."

But no one saw any pockets and word got around. Two days after the class, Jack was summoned to the President's office, to explain his teaching style. The President offered an explanation too, on the topic of Jack's freedom to pursue another job next semester.

So here they were. June had passed and between Jack's final check and some rather generous tips Diane had collected from the outgoing senior class, they managed to have July's rent and bills covered. August, however, was another matter, and they were going to have to figure out their next move.

Jack's going to have to figure out his next move, Diane corrected herself. She already had a move in mind. Hard as it may be.

A friend had once said to Diane, "Leave him, dear. He's a nice man, but he just isn't going to make it. You're going to be bartending all your life if you stay with him." She paused, this woman with a divorce under her belt and on the cusp of another, who lived in a large house, had drinks with friends every Thursday at four in the afternoon, and vacationed in Europe and Hong Kong, and then said, "You'll get tired. Eventually. You'll decide to move on. But if you're not careful, it'll be too late." Her friend took a long drag on her cigarette, a pull from her martini, and they both stared at the TV above the bar, the name or location of which Diane could no longer remember.

Then, and now: Diane knew he wouldn't make it. Not in the way they had always hoped. She didn't know when the end would come, but she knew it would come someday. He was too fragile. Or maybe that was too nice; maybe he was just an overeducated fuck-up.

"Hey Diane," Jack said, interrupting her reverie as he folded up the paper, "so what do you want to do today? You know, I think today is the perfect day for you and me just to hang out. Screw this job thing, something will come along. The Department Chair told me yesterday he heard there's an opening in the English Department at Elmira; he's got a friend there and is going to call the guy next week to see if I can get on the A list." He studied her face for a moment, then reached over and squeezed her hand. "Don't worry. We've always handled it before. I've changed now. It's been hard, but it's going to get better. Really. As long as I have you, we're going to make it."

Diane sighed again, straining against the tears. They escaped down her face anyway, and suddenly she couldn't hold it in and began to weep. Jack stood up and sat next to her, whispering, but she couldn't hear the words, only the concern in his voice. It was a dream now, the leaving, or maybe staying, but out of the corner of her eye she could see Miranda and a couple at another table staring at her, and she remembered how she didn't respond to her friend who told her to leave Jack. It came back now, the reason, and she could hear Jack's voice, as if from a distance, calling her, but she couldn't understand, she was curled up in a ball, beyond sadness, trying to shut out everything else and try to keep the moment, this feeling—maybe it wouldn't end well, maybe it would, but seeing it to the end was the reason she had to stay. She knew that now, always did, really, even if she'd forgotten it for a little while.

He needed her, and if it was her mission to hang in there until and through rock bottom, well, so be it. At least she knew it, she wasn't spinning around the planet chasing illusory happiness on the strength of alimony and gin, or counting on the realization of tightly held dreams of retirement bliss while the bulk of her life slipped away.

She thought of the road outside. Someone had told her that Rt. 20, in various incarnations through different states, stretched all the way to California. There had to be a lot of schools on Rt. 20, or whatever they called it in Ohio, Indiana, or other parts west. There had to be a lot of bars too, all looking for experienced help. It was enough hope for the future for her.

She'd keep the suitcase packed. But it wasn't leaving without Jack's to accompany it. Not today, anyway.

The Kindness of Strangers

I'm walking to the door of my apartment building. Moving quickly, and leaning into the February wind as it bare-teeth howls its way down the Albany streets. I'm carrying two plastic shopping bags full of weekend groceries, and although I've only just gotten out of the car, my fingers are already numb.

As I step into the doorway of my building, I see a man standing at the street corner. He is hunched over, arms wrapped around himself, staring at the ground. I watch him for almost a minute. He doesn't move, other than to tremble from the cold.

Then, on impulse, I walk over to him. "Do you need any help?" I ask.

He looks up, eyes unfocused, blinking.

"You're just standing there. Is there anything I can do to help?" This is awkward, but I wait for his answer.

"Got any money?" the man asks.

I reach in my pocket, feel some cash and pull out two twenties. I hesitate; I didn't plan on giving him that much. But his posture seems familiar, and suddenly I see the profile of another man; one who I last saw almost twenty years ago. As I hand over the cash, I wonder if it is as much restitution as generosity.

"Thanks, dude," the man says, and shuffles away.

Better late than never, I think.

❊ ❊ ❊

1987

We had been on the plane for nine hours and had nine more to go before we'd arrive in Tokyo. Refuel, then on to Hong Kong. From there, find our way to Beijing. Me, Kristine and Lori.

None of us could speak Chinese. I was a business major at SUNY Albany, ready to graduate the following semester. But the year before I had broken up with a longtime girlfriend, Georgia—"broken up" as in she dumped me, for reasons that aren't relevant and would not reflect well upon my character—and in a fit of college-boy despair I had decided to spend the fall of my senior year in China, full of romantic notions of forgetting her while seeing the world.

I had no idea what I was getting into. My family thought I was nuts. "Is it safe there, Jesse?" my mother would ask, never satisfied with an affirmative answer, despite such answer being given any number of times by any number of people. Since the actual trip was a year off when I had committed to going, I soon forgot about it and continued bumpily along through the rest of the school year and following summer, chasing Georgia to no avail until late August when she threw me out of a party at her house. It was her birthday party and I was not invited, so it was understandable. And that, as they say, was It.

Then came September, and all of a sudden I was on a plane and not coming back for four months. Up to that point, China was about as real as Mars; it wasn't as if I'd always dreamed of going there or even thought much about it. All I knew was that it was big. It was far away.

As for my traveling companions, I sort of knew Kristine; she used to date a buddy of mine. She was a native of Long Island, with an older sister who worked for MTV. Long, curly blonde hair and a great, if artificially enhanced, tan. Just-shy-of-spectacular body, and a wearer of white boots and jeans.

Lori was from SUNY Plattsburgh and she was short, I mean really short, 5'1" or something. She was skinny, with a dark complexion and straight black hair. She came from Jamestown, and it didn't seem that there was much money out in those parts, not to put too fine a point on it. She was nice enough, but a little uptight. During the flight she kept wanting to plan things to do and see while in Hong Kong. "It's our first exposure to another culture," she would say, "and I think we should make the most of it."

Finally Kristine turned to me and said, "Actually, Jimmy Brett—remember him, he bartends at the Hill Street Cafe? He told me to check out this place called 'Paradise Found'. It's supposed to have Mai Tai specials all day long. Cheesy karaoke too."

"Cool," I said.

Lori got the point and kept to herself after that.

We arrived before the serious jitters set in and I found myself wandering around the humid streets of Hong Kong, marveling at how strange everything was. It was similar to New York or any other western city: tall buildings, people in suits and sunglasses, McDonald's, cars zipping smartly about, the clash of smells and sounds. But the people in the suits were Asian, English was spoken only in scattered pockets between the rolling clips of Cantonese, the buildings were more colorful, and half the signs were in Mandarin. Nicely surreal, actually, if you got a whiskey buzz before wandering around.

It took us a day to figure out the best way to Beijing, about 1,100 miles north. We could fly, but Lori hinted—several times—that it was too expensive. I figured she should have thought of that before she signed up, but kept it to myself. A ship would take too long, and no one was up for renting a car and driving, if that was even possible. So we decided on the train. It would require an hour's scenic boat ride up the Pearl River to Guangzhou, on the other side of the border. From there, all we had to do was find the train station and we'd be off.

Guangzhou was a mildly unpleasant surprise. I'd assumed that like Hong Kong, the city would be ... modern. The difference was immediate. We got off the boat and walked boldly through customs, a shabby, lime green concrete structure with bored guards in military uniforms manning wooden tables, stamping our passports with careless thumps followed by brisk gestures to keep moving. No smiles or "welcome to China." No a/c, no fluorescent lights, no coffee shop, magazine shop, bar, gift shop or long, soft couches on which to recover one's reserves after a long night of Heinekens in a garish H.K. karaoke bar. There was only the open door through which the flies buzzed about, leading to the dusty street outside.

Walking over the cracked pavement, we quickly learned to stay well clear of the road, as the drivers seemed to consider traffic rules as polite but completely discretionary suggestions. Lori almost got nailed, stepping out to cross the street on a red light, jumping back just in time when she realized that the driver of a small truck that was overloaded with cabbage had no intention of letting a mechanical device dictate his behavior. Communist Party or no, the Chinese had fully embraced a chaotic form of automotive democracy entitling each to his or her own set of road-safety values.

It was also clear that the cool folks all lived in H.K., as the denizens of the Guangzhou streets all seemed to adopt a fashion best described as "Socialist Drab" in terms of style. Lots of nylon, bad sunglasses, all sandals.

There were no signs for any train station. At least none in English. We had just assumed that there'd be a clearly marked tram or bus or walkway that would lead us to the station and all would be hunky-dory in minutes. A half-hour's worth of trudging around the back streets of Guangzhou unburdened us of such notion, and Lori was getting seriously cranky about not being able to find a Coke machine. "I know they have fucking Coke; it was all over the news when they allowed them in a few years ago, remember? Maybe there's some inside here," she said, and she ran into some sort of commercial establishment, its nature not clear other than a hand-painted, battered wooden sign leaning against the flaking wall by the door. She soon came back out, looking scared.

It wasn't the contents of the store that scared her, "cooking stuff, I think," she muttered, but the fact that indeed, she might be so far from home that there was no Coca-Cola available. I thought she was going to cry, and Kristine and I walked silently ahead to give her some space.

I was getting worried, too. It was a ridiculous problem but we just couldn't find the station, nor could we find anyone to ask; our several attempts causing no small amount of confusion. One person we seemed to have somehow offended, as he sputtered indignantly and stomped away. Eventually I settled on the idea of sticking two fingers on one hand out like a horizontal peace sign and running the other hand over them while saying, "choo-choo, choo-choo." When my little performance was over, I'd put a hand over my eyes and pretend to scan the horizon, then hope that the befuddled stranger we'd accosted had understood.

We hit pay dirt on the second try, the woman instantly aware of our dilemma, and in a burst of enthusiasm gave us detailed directions to the train station.

It was all in Chinese, of course.

I was starting to wonder if it was too late to catch a boat back to Hong Kong, when a Chinese gentleman walked up to us. He was young, in his late twenties, wearing cargo pants, sneakers and a green jacket with a Kinks T-shirt underneath. He had a black fisherman's cap with a red communist star affixed to the front above the brim, and round, gold-framed glasses, like John Lennon's. A bit shorter than me, with thick, black hair. I started in again with the whole "choo-choo" thing when he held up a hand.

"Yeah, I know. Follow me," he said with a slight British accent, and started walking.

We looked at each other and hurried after him. He was laughing when we caught up. "I saw you talking to that lady over there. Good idea, but you have to be able to understand the directions!"

"Well, glad you came along, we were just about out of ideas," Kristine said. "I was thinking we might have to go back."

"So was I," said Lori, in a tone that suggested it was still a viable plan to her.

"Can't go back now, the last boat left half an hour ago. Where are you going, anyway?" he asked.

"Beijing," we answered in unison.

"Well, so am I. What for?"

"School," Kristine replied, "We're there for the semester."

He smiled. "And again, so am I. Which school?"

I pulled out one of the several slips of paper the folks at Albany had given me. It was covered with Chinese characters, and apparently identified me as a student trying to get to Beijing; offered the name of the school and its address; and listed my allergies and contact information should something go awry.

He studied the paper. "Shifan Xueuan. That's Beijing Teacher's College. I thought it would be Beijing University; that's where they usually put the foreigners."

"Is it a good school?" Lori asked.

"I don't know. I mean, if you want to be a teacher, you could go there, but there are a lot of schools like that. I've heard of it. It's small, that's all I know."

"Where are you going?" I asked.

"Beijing University. To study electrical engineering."

"Where are you from?" Kristine asked.

"Hong Kong. And my name is Peter Li." He stuck out his hand first to Kristine, and then shook all our hands as we introduced ourselves.

"Your English is so good," Lori said, "I thought you were from the US."

"We speak English in Hong Kong too," he said. "My father worked for the British consulate, so he had to speak it."

"What did he do?" Lori asked, "Was he an ambassador or something?"

Peter smiled and said, "He cleaned the offices."

As we approached the train station, Peter said, "Look, if you don't mind, I'll do the talking. They'll take advantage of you, try to put you in an over-priced, first class cabin." He paused. "I'm assuming you don't want that. I mean, if that's fine with—"

"No, no, please, whatever you recommend," Lori broke in.

I sighed. I had loads of cash and liked the phrase, "first class." But I just shut up and nodded.

"Well then," Peter said, "second class it is. Each cabin has four bunks, so you might end up sharing with someone. But it'll be clean and much cheaper."

"OK," I said, "sounds like a plan."

"Right, "he said, "Ah, if you each give me ... " He turned to look at the sign above the line of teller windows. "Give me 70 yuan each, I'll get your tickets."

Suddenly I was a little concerned about giving him the money. It would have been the perfect scam to play on a bunch of fool American college kids. I could tell Kristine was thinking the same thing by the look on her face. Lori seemed as happy as could be.

Peter must have picked up on our thoughts; he looked embarrassed and kept his eyes down. Not at all the sort of behavior I'd expect from a guy who was going to rip me off—I've had it happen, and they are much more cheerful—and I felt guilty for suspecting him as I handed over my cash.

Peter was walking to the nearest window when Lori called out, "Why aren't you going to take the fourth bunk?"

He stopped and turned. "I need to save my money; I'm taking 3rd class." Then he grinned. "It's all right; I will have friends in high places."

✼ ✼ ✼

"God, it's hot," Lori said, for the fifth or sixth time. She was sitting on the bunk opposite Kristine and me. In Hong Kong we went from air-conditioned hotel rooms to air-conditioned bars, via air-conditioned cabs. I had assumed the Chinese would resist the raging heat with the same technological vigor. By providing air-conditioned trains, for example.

I learned that they just sweat.

82

We were all staring out the window as the train lurched its way down the tracks, drinking the beer that Peter had recommended. "Chinese beer is very cheap," Peter told us. "You'll like it."

It was pretty good, and six quart-size bottles cost about $4 at the station kiosk. Our first effort at a meal was less successful. Shortly after the train started moving, a man in a uniform came by and handed us what appeared to be menus, then stood there, pen and pad in hand, smiling and nodding as we pondered the indecipherable characters smudgily printed on the rough paper. We had to choose something, and in the end randomly pointed to whatever gibberish looked like it had potential (there was a certain character that I had come to believe, based on nothing other than its interesting shape, represented moo-shoo pork).

What came back was a small piece of pickled cabbage (not bad), two bowls of very thin soup (watery), and something chicken-based, complete with bones and organs (untouched and covered up). We split the cabbage, I sipped some of the soup, and then we all sat back and stared out the window into the twilight, wondering if we could survive the three-day train ride to Beijing on just pickled cabbage.

Our contemplations were interrupted by a knock at the door of our compartment, and it slid open.

"Peter!" Lori said, "Please, come in. How are you?"

"Fine, fine," he said, sitting down next to her. "How are you guys doing?"

We related the story of our failed dinner and he chuckled. "Yeah, you're not going to get any American hamburgers on this ride, and certainly no menus in English. If it helps, I'd be happy to translate for you next time."

We agreed that this was a wonderful idea, offering to buy his meals in exchange for such services.

"No, no, I just want to help, you don't have to do that." But we insisted and without much prodding, he agreed. I think he was relieved; I couldn't help but notice that he only carried a small black nylon duffel bag containing his belongings for a semester. Altogether, the three of us had eight or nine bags, all of them larger, better quality and representing a sacrifice of the possessions that didn't fit.

"Why don't you just stay here, Peter? No one else took the forth bunk. We don't mind, really," Kristine said.

"You don't understand. You are strangers, they don't get many meiguorens—Americans—on the train here. They'll be checking on you just out of curiosity, and they'll certainly look at my ticket. If I'm found sleeping here, they'll throw me off the train."

And so it was agreed that for the rest of the trip Peter would remain with us during the day and sleep in his 3rd class car at night.

It worked out great. At meal times, he would read from the menu, offer recommendations, and order for us. The food was O.K., sufficient at least to stave off hunger until we rolled into Beijing Station.

The second night, after Kristine and Lori had dozed off, I got out of bed and headed to where Peter said his car was located. I went through two second-class cars like ours, staggering with the roll of the train as I made my way down the aisle, passing couples and families who were stretched out on bunks, reading books, idly smoking or just watching the countryside go by. I passed between cars for the third time, wincing at the roar from the tracks below, and opened the door to the third-class car.

It was dark, lit only by a few bare bulbs affixed along one wall of the car. Wooden benches with low backs lined either side of the center aisle, people packed four or five deep on each bench. About half were sleeping, slumped against their neighbor with their belongings sitting between their legs, covered by a protective hand. It was very hot; everyone was sweating, and I felt instantly awash in my fellow traveler's fluids.

Most of the other half seemed to be drinking; copious amounts of beer flowed into throats, onto shirts, the floor, the pant legs of slumbering neighbors. All of them were smoking. Aggressively so, sucking hard on their cigarettes, creating a dense cloud that the open windows could do little to dispel. Although everyone was trying to be quiet, their joint effort at hushed conversation created a din that complemented the mechanical clanking of the train's wheels on the tracks.

I didn't see any other foreigners. A couple of guys smiled and said something to me, I could only grin and nod back. Someone handed me a beer, and I smiled even broader and thanked him, causing much mirth among his friends. Sipping the warm beer I scanned the faces for Peter, eventually finding him in the back, facing me, head resting on the shoulder of an elderly man who was calmly smoking a cigarette and staring back at me. Peter's mouth was open and he coughed in his sleep, hunching over and hacking audibly before returning to his original position.

I raised my bottle to the guys who had given it to me, offering a bad "zai jian"—goodbye. They tried to get me to stay, gesturing for me to join them. But I didn't want Peter to know that I'd seen him; it seemed too intimate a view of our discrepancy of lodgings. I returned to our compartment where the girls were sleeping and watched the fields go by in the moonlight.

It was early afternoon and raining when we neared Beijing. We were watching the flat fields slowly give way to small brick houses held together with crumbling mortar, and soon the dirt roads became paved, the houses replaced by two and three story cement apartments.

Suddenly, the train lurched to a halt and Lori asked, "Are we there yet?"

"I don't think so," said Peter. "We're still on the outskirts."

I sat back and cracked a beer. Peter rejected my offer for one, as he had throughout our trip, instead taking occasional sips of tea from a red flask that seemed to last him an entire day. The girls gave me a look, suddenly all prim, but after an hour of sitting there they had begun to drink too.

We got into a discussion of our favorite bands—Peter was very knowledgeable about western music, pulling a Replacements reference out of nowhere—and we were arguing about whether hair metal had any merit when suddenly a woman in a blue uniform appeared in front of us. She was small, with flecks of grey in her black hair, but carried an air of martial authority as she glanced at us. In a sharp tone, she said something to Peter. He replied softly, gesturing at us, but she shook her head and repeated whatever it was, only louder. Peter stared at her for a moment, then sighed.

"I can't stay here. I don't have a second class ticket."

"But we're your friends. It's not like you're sleeping here or anything," Lori said.

"I know, but you don't understand—" he was cut off by the woman's repeated demand, and she took a step into the cabin to tug at Peter's sleeve.

"No, wait!" Kristine said.

Lori was nodding her head and pointing at Peter, repeating, "It's OK, it's OK."

But the woman only smiled at us—a sudden and truly wonderful smile, a "welcome-to-our-city" smile if I ever saw one, and for a moment I thought everything was going to be all right. Until she turned and barked even louder at Peter.

Peter stood up. "OK, I have to go. Sorry." He rubbed his eyes with the palms of his hands. "I'll see you guys when we get off."

"But why now? You've been here the whole trip! We're getting off soon, what's the difference?" Lori asked, but he was already gone, escorted down the aisle by the woman.

The train sat for another two hours, then began to crawl ahead, arriving at the station just before midnight. I was regretting the beer, by this time I'd had more than a few and was a little tired. I couldn't remember where I'd put the directions to the school, and was wondering how we were going to get there anyway.

"Where's Peter?" Lori asked as we carried our belongings off the train and onto the platform. "We don't have his address or number or anything. I thought he'd catch up to us."

"I did," a tired voice said, and there he was behind us, carrying the small duffle, looking as if he'd spent the intervening hours sleeping underneath the train. His clothes were rumpled and there were dark circles under his eyes, but he was still smiling.

We explained our dilemma while walking out of the station onto the street, the crowd of fellow-travelers quickly disappearing into waiting cars or walking off into darkness as a light rain fell. Unlike every other city I'd known, Beijing was distinctly quiet at night. Few cars terrorized the roads, and there were only a handful of people riding by on bicycles, ignoring the drizzle as they pedaled by with plastic bags hanging from handlebars or boxes strapped to rear fenders.

"Didn't your school make arrangements?" Peter asked.

"They gave us these." Kristine pulled a note out of her backpack, handing it to him.

"It asks the reader to guide you to a cab and tell the driver to take you to Shifan Xueyuan. Not a bad idea, most people will help you out." He looked around. "Assuming, of course that there are cabs available to take you there."

"Well, how were you going to get to your school?" I asked.

"Walk, actually. Beijing University is only a couple of miles away."

"Do you know where Surefan Shu ... our school is?" Kristine asked.

"No," he replied, "but that will help." He pointed towards a large map set behind a plastic shield that was screwed into the outer wall of the station and we groggily shuffled after him.

After studying the map, he frowned and said, "It's too far to walk. You need a cab."

We all turned to face the empty street. "Shit," I said.

"Wait here," Peter said, "Let me see what I can do," and he went inside the station.

"What would we do without him?" Lori asked. "They didn't prepare us at all for any of this."

I sighed. I had to go to the bathroom, and scanned the building's exterior for sign of a men's room. Nothing. I decided that I couldn't wait and went inside. Peter was talking to a guard, who was shaking his head. Peter reached into his pocket and handed him money. The guard paused, then turned and walked away, heading towards the door of what appeared to be an office.

Peter saw me and came over. "A cab will be coming in a bit."

"Yeah, thanks. Um, what do we owe you? I saw you give that guy money."

"Oh, that's all right Jesse," he said.

"No really, I don't mind, I appreciate the help." I started snapping my fingers and tapping my foot, all jittery and anxious. I had to go bad now, and would give him whatever, after I took care of more pressing business.

"Well," he began.

"Is there a bathroom around here?" I broke in. "I really gotta go."

He looked around, then pointed to a doorway at the opposite side of the room. "There."

"Thanks," I said, and half-ran for it.

� ✻ ✻ ✻

The cab pulled up in front of the school's gate and a guard stepped out. There were a lot of guards in China. Not that they were necessarily needed; it was a very law abiding country. But there were so many people to provide jobs for, the government apparently decided to guard every building, park, newsstand and large tree.

Peter leaned out of the cab and said something to the man, who then turned and opened the gate, motioning us inside. I was exhausted, Kristine had nodded off and Lori was getting short-tempered, having already chastised me for lowering the window in the cab and letting in the rain.

I didn't mind though. I had been contemplating my future with Kristine; during the last few hours on the train, she had been touching my arm and leg whenever she spoke to me, and had provided a quick back massage, promising a "much better one"—complete with a wink—when we were settled in.

We got out, hefted our luggage, then turned to the cab. "Peter, do you have an address or a number?" Lori asked.

"No," he said, "Not yet. But I'll stop by in a few days."

"How will you find us? You don't know what dorm we are in."

Peter smiled. "It won't be hard to find the Americans. The school officials will know where you are."

"Peter, thanks for everything," I said. "Ladies, I'm beat." As I turned towards the gate, I heard Lori and Kristine say their thank you's and good-bye's.

Following the guard as we walked towards the nearest building, I heard Lori say out loud, "Oh! We stuck him with the cab fare."

And a twinge; I forgot to repay him for the money he gave to the guard at the train station.

The Dean of the school had been waiting for us, and in fairly good English she offered a welcome, complete with tea and biscuits, then showed us to our rooms. We were on a floor that housed four other Americans, who were in the midst of a party when we arrived. Two girls, Annette and Jackie—cute and less cute, both dark haired, large breasts and piles of money, judging by their clothes and jewelry—were from Colgate. One guy, Ryan, was from some school in Pennsylvania (quiet and good looking to the point of competition, possible jerk). The other guy, Matt (obvious stoner) was from Bowdoin. The Dean admonished them for drinking too much and having the music too loud, although I sighed with relief when I heard The Police. I had forgotten to pack my tapes. But she soon left us to resume the party in full, if slightly muted, swing.

We told the tale of our journey; it was much longer than theirs as they had all flown directly to Beijing and were picked up by a limo.

"Sounds like you guys had a pretty cool adventure," Matt said. "I wish I'd done it that way."

"We were lucky," I reminded him. "Without Peter it wouldn't have been much fun."

"Yeah," he agreed. "So, you guys smoke? Hash is fucking cheap here!" he said as he pulled out the bong stashed under his bed.

※　※　※

The strange environment, the fact that we all were in the same classes, went on the same tours of museums, to plays, historic sites and so on, created a bond fairly quickly, and time passed even faster than the normal whoosh of youth. Kristine flirted a lot with Ryan at first, but something happened by the end of the first week and she was flirting with me again by the second week, sleeping with me by the third week. It had taken a little longer than I had thought, but she eventually stopped by for that special massage.

I hung out a lot with Matt; we shared the same tastes in music, beer and weed. With respect to the latter, while at first I couldn't take a hit without reruns of "Midnight Express" running through my head, a few days worth dissipated any fear of official reprisal. "They don't know what it is, I swear," he told me one night. "They think they are American cigarettes. I told the cleaning girl they were clove, an American thing."

It was the end of the first month and I was lying in bed on a Friday afternoon, listening to Matt's "Making Movies" tape and staring at the ceiling. There was a knock on the door, and I thought it was Annette, who despite my obvious

88

relationship with Kristine, was acting very friendly, often coming into my room when Kristine wasn't around, to "chat." Sometimes wearing only a black athletic bra and silk boxers. It was nice, and being a former Boy Scout, I didn't discourage her. Best to be prepared in case of unexpected need.

But when I opened the door, Peter was standing in front of me. He was wearing the exact same clothes as when I'd last seen him. Clean. Just the same.

"Hello Jesse. How are you?" he asked.

"Great, great. Come on in," I said, pointing to the bed. "Have a seat."

He sat down, looking around at the drawings and flyers I had taped to the walls.

"You like Chinese art?" he asked.

"Yeah, actually. It's pretty cool stuff."

He frowned, looking at a flyer with a swan logo on it. "You like Chinese tools?" He asked.

"What?"

He pointed to the flyer. "You have an ad for a tool sale at the Chaoyang Factory. Special on wrenches."

I laughed. "No, no, I just liked the picture of the bird."

Lori, walking past my room, saw Peter and got Kristine and everyone else, gathering them in a semicircle around him. "This is the guy," she said proudly, her arm around him, "The guy who saved us!" Peter grinned and looked down as she reiterated the tale of our journey north. To my slight annoyance, she left out the part about my clever imitation of a train, which I felt would've gotten us there sooner or later. When she finished, there were some nods, a "way to go," then a moment of silence.

"So, who's hungry?" Annette asked.

"Right," said Ryan. Jackie was already walking out the door to get her coat. They had been a couple from the start, and never went anywhere without the other.

"Peter, come to dinner with us," Lori said.

He hesitated. "I just wanted to say hello. I didn't plan on going out."

I noticed bags under his eyes. He was smiling easily enough, but there was an air of fatigue about him.

"Partying too much?" I asked. "Hanging out with a wild crowd?"

"No," he sighed. "I don't have many friends here. Most of my classmates live with their parents; we don't socialize much in school."

"Got to get yourself a babe," I said, receiving a swat from Kristine. "Ease your mind."

He looked at me, his face serious. "Not here. I don't have any money. The girls at my school don't want to date the son of a laborer. Maybe after I get my degree and get a job. Not now."

I was only trying to lighten the mood, but let it go.

"So. Where we gonna go? Try something local?" Matt asked.

"I'm told there's a nice place not far from here," Peter said.

We looked at him. "I can show you," he said.

"Cool," Matt said. "Lead the way, Peter my friend."

It was a short distance, but we never would have found it on our own. Peter lead us several blocks down the street from the school, then turned into an alleyway. We walked to the end, turned right and went another few yards down a narrow street lined with tiny homes, most of them made of stacked brick, no mortar or anything. As we passed an open door I saw a single room with a bed against the far wall. There was a couple huddled over a small kerosene heater, and a child standing in front of the bed, playing with some string. It looked like they had a few things on some crude shelves, pots and pans and such, but the place was otherwise bare.

Peter turned and walked through the narrow stone doorway of a slightly larger concrete structure. Following, we entered a rather nice, vaguely western-looking restaurant. There was a bar, and tables and chairs that matched. Not that I ordinarily cared about such things, but you tend to be more observant when everything that's usually different starts to look familiar again.

"Well," Peter said, "I think you'll like this. I found it a few weeks ago when I was looking for you," and he glanced at Kristine and Lori and me, "but no one was around. I got to wandering, saw this place, and ... " He gestured to the door. "Anyway, I wasn't planning on eating, so I think I'm going to—"

"Wait!" Lori said. "Peter, you have to join us."

"Well ... "

"We'll pay," Kristine said.

He hesitated long enough to pretend that wasn't the issue, then, "OK, if you don't mind."

Peter resumed his role as guide and ordered for the table. We bought round after round of Beijing beer, punctuated by several courses of what turned out to be excellent food—spicy noodles with lentils, some Mongolian hot pot beef (cooked in an ornate silver boiler that sat at the center of the table), rice with steamed vegetables in peanut sauce, dumplings and some sort of sweet yogurt-thing for dessert. And more beer. The whole deal cost us about $5 apiece, and we stumbled out several hours later, quite drunk, happy and ready to resume the party back at my room.

"Hey Peter, why don't you come with us?" Lori asked, but Matt shushed her.

"What?" I heard her whisper. Peter was several steps ahead, apparently oblivious.

"Well, you know, the weed and all," Matt said.

"What about it?" She demanded.

"Well, I don't know him, you know? Don't want to go looking for trouble."

"I thought you said they think they're clove cigarettes," I said out of the corner of my mouth.

"Yes, the folks from here think it's clove," he replied. "Most do, anyway," he added, alluding to a close call with the police while riding a bus a few weeks back. "But your buddy is from Hong Kong. They know about it there."

"No problem," Lori said. "Don't smoke. Peter!" She called out again, "Come with us!"

He turned around. The smile was still there, but faded, and he looked at Matt before he said, softly, "No, thank you. I have to study. Big test tomorrow."

"But tomorrow's a Saturday."

"Yes," he replied. "See you soon. Maybe we can go get some coffee somewhere."

"Great idea," Matt called over his shoulder; he was already walking away.

"Yeah, coffee," Annette said, following Matt. Ryan and Jackie were also on their way.

I mumbled something and turned away. I should've hung out with him, offered to go for coffee right then, but ... Kristine had been rubbing my leg between dessert and the final beer, and it had been a couple of days, at least. I was looking forward to some of Matt's weed and quality time with Kristine.

✖ ✖ ✖

Another month went by. By this time, Kristine and I weren't getting along, which was a drag. She was seeing this guy we had met at a hotel bar, some Aussie who worked at the embassy. But Annette and I were increasingly friendly, and I had much optimism with respect to our relationship.

I was walking around the city one afternoon, bored. My classes were a bit dry and the tests were easy, so I figured attendance was optional. Besides, I was here to "absorb the culture," not listen to someone yap on about a series of eight hundred year old power struggles by a bunch of psychopathic horsemen.

Hands stuffed into a new leather trench coat, wraparound shades in place and grooving to some Lou Reed on Matt's Walkman, I was looking for a coffee shop, the "Imperial Palace." It was supposed to be a decent joint that catered to Westerners. I was told that it also provided hash for those in the know, or so Matt had heard from some guy he knew from another school. I had invited him along, but he had been absorbing the culture more than I of late, and needed to study to pass a makeup.

Suddenly, I saw Peter. He was standing outside a small shop, eating a cup of yogurt. He looked a bit thinner. Same clothes, still, but there was a stain on the pants and his jacket was wrinkled. Half the collar was twisted up; whether he didn't notice or didn't care I couldn't tell.

"Hey Peter," I called, pulling off the headphones.

He looked up, seemingly alarmed, then saw who it was and relaxed. "Jesse."

"What's up, guy? How are things?"

"OK," he said. "How are you?"

"Fine, fine. Having a blast. How's school?"

He paused. "I'm taking a break at the moment. My parents were supposed to send the rest of the tuition money last week, but it never came."

"Whew! You want to give them a call, get on top of that."

"They don't have a telephone, Jesse," he said. His voice was oddly quiet. "I sent them a telegram and am waiting to hear back."

"So, what, the school won't let you in class until you pay?"

"No. I can't come on campus at all until I pay."

"Yikes," I said. "So hey, how about that cup of coffee? I buy," I said to avoid any awkwardness. I figured he'd have to save his cash.

"That would be nice," he said.

"OK. Ah, how about 6:00 tonight? Marriott Hotel on Xisanhuan Beilu?"

Peter hesitated. "They … discourage Chinese from going there. Foreigners only."

"But you're from Hong Kong … "

"It is a distinction a bit fine for them, I'm afraid."

"But you're my guest. Wait. I'll meet you out front, and we can go in together, you'll be my guest. You gotta try it, the coffee's great," I said. "Best in town."

He paused again, then said, "OK, Jesse. If you really want to."

"Fantastic!" I said. "Gotta go." Annette was done with class in about an hour, and I thought that perhaps we could hang out in my room for awhile. See what might develop.

"Bye, Jesse," he said.

"See you later, dude," and I slapped him on the shoulder. "Zijian-a!"

An hour and a half later, things had developed better than I had hoped. Annette's demonstration of affection was nothing short of enthusiastic; seems she felt like she had to make up for lost time. All intentions of going anywhere diminished with every whack of the bed against the wall.

I woke up a little after six that evening, saw the time and said, "Shit."

"What?" Annette asked. She was lying half on top of me. It felt great.

"I was supposed to meet Peter at the Marriot."

"Oh," she yawned, "your friend from the train?"

"Yeah."

"When?"

"Sort of now."

"Hmmm," and she was silent, breathing deeply almost immediately.

I should go, I thought. Throw on my sweats and get a cab. But then Annette started to caress my thigh. Turned out she wasn't really sleepy after all.

In class the next day, I told Lori about seeing Peter and forgetting to meet him for coffee, although I left out the details as to exactly why.

"Yes Jesse, sex will do that," she replied, and I was reminded of how small our expat community really was.

"We oughta see him some time. I don't think things are going well for him."

"I know," she sighed. "Kristine ran into him last week. He's been staying in some dollar-a-night place. She thinks it might be the basement of one of those factories that lets people sleep on their grungy floor. Isn't that illegal? She said there's a lot of TB spread in those places." Lori bit her lip. "Do you think he needs help?"

I didn't know. What were we supposed to do? Give him money? Let him stay with us? I'd have to sleep in Annette's room, which wasn't bad in itself, but still, there was the hassle of someone in my room. Loaning him cash wasn't a problem per se, but I'd have to cut back on my expenses a bit if I gave him some, and I had planned some serious fun with the money I had.

"What does Kristine think?" I asked.

"She was going to go see him the other night and have a talk, but I guess her Aussie friend wanted her to go to some function with him."

"Do you know where he is? How we can find him?"

"Kristine knows," she said. I nodded my head, thinking that Lori would report our conversation to Kristine, who was in possession of the most useful information, and a plan would be formulated from there. Someone would get back to me with the details. I'd help where I could.

But Lori, I'm sure, assumed that I'd talk to Kristine, and that we would form the plan from there. I guess. Who knows? We had agreed that he needed help, that we were the ones to help him, and just moved on. Annette and I went to Tianjin for the weekend. Kristine and Lori did their own thing. Peter just did whatever he had to do.

I saw Peter only one time after that. Three couples—me and Annette, Matt and some girl from another school, Kristine and her Aussie—had rented a limo and were riding around one night, drinking the Jack Daniels that Matt's cousin had illegally mailed from the States, hitting all the spots that we had managed to unearth over the semester. We had some regular club friends, mostly young embassy-types or kids from other schools, and we had managed to create for ourselves a nice, jet-setty little world. We were on our way to "The Great Wall," a new jazz bar owned by a Chinese-American from Boston who was making a go of it with some relatives. It was cold, winters in Beijing are as cold as upstate New York, maybe colder. But we were fortified against the elements in our black limo, with some Grateful Dead on the stereo and the JD, balanced nicely with hits from the bong that Matt had made out of bamboo and an empty soy sauce jar.

It was about 11:00 pm, and we were at a traffic light. The wind was so strong it was causing the light to sway on the wire. I was staring out the window, nodding my head to "Playing in the Band" and zoning. Annette sat on my lap, wiggling nicely now and then, talking to Matt about the best places to visit before we went home. Matt wanted to go to Thailand; he heard that it was some sort of adult Disneyland, while Annette said she was thinking about taking the trans-Siberian railroad from Vladivostok to Moscow, look around for a bit, then home via Paris. She wasn't very clear on how to get to Vladivostok from Beijing, but I didn't bother to point that out. It didn't matter, Annette was just talking. I knew she had already bought a ticket for a flight straight home from Beijing. We hadn't discussed the issue of what we were going to do when we got back. Although we were having a good time together, I think we both wanted to keep our options open. I did, anyway.

I had been thinking a lot about my options. Option, actually. Potential option, really. Wondering if Georgia really meant it when she said she never wanted to see me again. Screamed it, to be accurate, but after sucker-punching the guy who had just given her a birthday kiss—his status as her current boyfriend notwithstanding—I had to admit it was a possibility.

Then I saw Peter at a bus stop.

The buses don't run all night in Beijing, and he must've been waiting for the last one. He was alone. Same clothes, but his pants were ripped above the right knee. He had on a knit cap and a scarf, maybe a turtleneck under the dirty green jacket, but no way was he warm. Even from a distance I could see him shivering, and he hunched over to cough, practically hacking his guts out. Out of the corner of my eye I could also see Annette pulling off her sweater—the wonderful shape of those breasts forcing a full glance—and I heard her complaining about the

94

heat. I looked back and Peter was weaving a little. I wondered if he was drunk. Then he leaned against a light pole, folded his arms and stared at the ground.

I just sat there until the light changed and the car pulled ahead. I looked past Matt, at Kristine who was sitting next to the opposite door. She had to have seen him too. But she was staring, hard, at the floor of the limo, her lips pursed in concentration.

We had a party to go to.

� ✖ ✖

That was it. The party was a good one; they were all good, and they lasted another two weeks, one every night, until I flew back to New York.

I don't know what happened to Peter. I did try to see him again, two days before I left. It was right after I'd broken up, somewhat inartfully, with Annette. The inartful part involved her finding me in bed with Kristine as a sort of "fare-well" gesture. Annette was crying, weeping actually, asking me how I could be so awful—didn't I know what I meant to her?

It was the same sort of thing Georgia had said to me, the last time I'd made a similar gesture with someone else.

The next morning, hung over, feeling guilty, I got the address of the place where Kristine thought Peter was staying. It took almost an hour by bus, to the edge of the city, and another 30 minutes walking in the rain, wandering through a maze of dirty back streets that spliced clusters of smoke-retching industrial plants and small chemical shops.

It was a three-story brick building, tucked down an alleyway behind what appeared to be a paint shop. I went through a crooked doorway into a large room, bare but for a couple of broken chairs at one end and a pile of foul-smelling cans at the other. A few workers shambled in from a doorway at the opposite end of the room, heading for the street, but no one stopped to give me a second look, not even when I pleaded, in my bad, bar-learned Chinese, if anyone had seen or even heard of Peter. I only got, "bu"—no—and a listless shake of the head. They didn't even break stride.

I walked around the neighborhood for a while, looking for a glimpse of him, hoping for one more chance encounter, where the luck of a friend's benevolence would flow his way for a change. I had money, $500, and was going to give it to him for decent shelter, a train ticket home, a good meal, whatever.

I never found him, of course, and as the overcast sky turned dark, the dull fatigue of homebound laborers was replaced by the more interested and slightly feral stares from the deepening shadows. I left and halfway home found a bar. I don't remember getting back. Seems I spent almost all the money, though.

✖ ✖ ✖

I got back together with Georgia a month after I returned to the states. Finished my senior year and we got married. We stayed in Albany, started careers, had kids, the whole thing. I got a job with a bank, starting out as a midlevel manager and ended up doing all right for myself. Survived two buy-outs and a merger; a higher salary and fancier title every time we changed the name above the front door. The recession? Hey, someone had to make money on all those collateralized debt obligations. The view of my financial outlook now requires sunglasses.

We got divorced last year. It was hard. It wasn't my fault, although most of my friends didn't believe it until they got independent confirmation. My kids live with her and her new friend in our house. Her house, technically. I let her have the dog too. That was a mistake. My apartment is too quiet.

I've learned some things.

I pour a whiskey and sit down, leaving the groceries in the hallway. I haven't even taken off my coat; I just want to think.

I wonder how Peter made out. Not well, I know that now. I knew it then. Stranded on the streets of Beijing, too poor to get home or to send a message for help. It was harder than most people here can understand. Maybe he got thrown in jail for vagrancy; it was a common solution to homelessness. Maybe he got sick. Either way, he might as well have been stranded in the desert.

Tomorrow, maybe I'll do something. I have lots of time this weekend. Most weekends. Maybe I'll volunteer at a homeless shelter. I should donate to a charity; I have the means to make a difference.

I'm a little lost, now. That guy on the street is lost, in a more fundamental way. Peter was lost, alone and at the mercy of callous souls he mistook for friends. I think about my children, and hope they never have to seek favor from an indifferent heaven.

I owe Peter something. The money I gave to the guy outside is a start. A measure of kindness to strangers, the best I'm able, offered as an apology for the kindness that I never bothered to offer him. It won't repay the debt, but I hope it mitigates the interest on my conscience.

Fall Harvest

Carter set his glasses on the desk and rubbed his eyes. It was time to call it a day; he had to get going soon. He put the glasses back on, pushing the bridge to the top of his nose with his finger, and spun his chair around to look out the window behind him.

It was getting dark, the sun having begun to retire earlier each day as October carried the season to its colder end. Carter studied his reflection in the glass; a thin figure with a rumpled shirt and rolled up sleeves staring back at him. He looked younger than he was though, or so it seemed, the window giving him back a good ten years—mid 40's, tops. He straightened his tie, sighed, then loosened it.

His office, on the 15h floor of a tower in Chicago's North Loop, overlooked Lakeshore Drive and Lake Michigan beyond. In the remaining light he could see the whitecaps push their way across the water. Something about the water's progress reminded him of his pending travel. The leaves should be turning, he thought, maybe I should bring a camera.

Carter hadn't slept well the past few days, and was counting on the flight to get a decent nap in. A drink or two at the airport would help; there was a nice little bar there, dark, with high-backed stools and music turned low, perfect for calming jitters. Designed for flying-jitters, actually, not necessarily those Carter was feeling, but then again alcohol covered the full jitter-spectrum regardless.

He sighed again and stood up; it was time to get moving. He had brought his suitcase to work and was going to take a cab straight to O'Hare.

"All set to go, Carter?" his secretary, Brenda, asked as he passed her desk on his way to the door.

"Hope so."

She sat back in her chair and looked at him thoughtfully. "What's wrong? You've been quiet all day. I thought you were going to your hometown."

"I am."

"Sorry, I know I just asked this—Vermont or New Hampshire?"

"Luther, Vermont. Up near the Canadian border."

"That's it, right, I remember. Just east of nowhere."

"North of it, actually."

"Gonna stay with family?"

Carter shook his head. "My mother lives in Florida. My father passed away years ago."

"Brothers or sisters?"

"Got a sister in Massachusetts. An aunt and a couple of cousins too, but they are all in L.A. Haven't seen any of them in years."

"No one left back home—that's going to be a little weird. Do you keep in touch with any old friends?"

"Not really."

She paused, waiting for him to explain, then, "Well, still. A small town, right? You must know half the people there."

"You'd think."

"When's the last time you were back?"

He looked up at the ceiling, scanning the tiles. "Not sure. About fifteen, twenty years ago."

"Huh. That's a long time."

"Yeah." Carter looked at his watch, then back to Brenda. She was waiting for more. "Well, you know, I just never made it back after college. My parents moved during my last year in school, so there wasn't really a 'home' anymore, I guess. Always meant to go back, but things just kept coming up."

She squinted at him. "Things."

"Yup."

"Ok. Tell me about it when you get back." She turned back to her keyboard and started typing.

"Well, I should get going, so .... "

"Safe travels, Carter."

"Thanks."

Two hours later, on the plane heading east, he thought about what he didn't tell her, what she clearly expected to hear when he got back—that for the life of him, he just didn't know why, exactly why, he never went back. Years ago, before he stopped even pretending that someday he'd return, he would schedule a weekend or a few days of vacation time for a visit to Luther. But inevitably something came up at work, or his wife or girlfriend or (many years ago) a drinking buddy would have a better plan and the trip got canceled. He'd blown off so many invitations—get-togethers with old friends, weddings, class reunions, a couple of funerals even.

Then one day, it was just too late to return. He had crossed some threshold he hadn't known existed until he looked behind him. Carter didn't mind, not much anyway. The feeling was odd, but not necessarily bad. Not as long as he didn't think too much about it, and there wasn't much in Chicago to remind him of Vermont.

Since last year his company, DairyTek, had been on an acquisition spree, targeting failing creameries in the Northeast and snapping them up right before they went under. As VP of Risk Management, it was his job to visit recent purchases. He'd meet with the on-site executive team and go over state and federal regulations, insurance issues, pending litigation, labor matters and the like. He'd been to upstate New York, all over Pennsylvania, a few towns in Massachusetts—before each trip he would idly consider a brief excursion north to Luther, then quickly dismiss it for lack of time.

But last month he learned that DairyTek had bought Luther Creamery, Inc. Carter had forgotten about the place, he had just assumed that it had long since disappeared. But it hadn't, its slow decline positioning it to land in DairyTek's arms, and now he had to do the standard review.

Ordinarily, it would be just another quick initial visit to make sure everyone knew the direction they were supposed to go and who they could call for help. Carter had read the list of names of the senior staff; to his relief he didn't recognize anyone. Still, the prospect made him uneasy. It was like coming back as a stranger, with someone else's past that had to be honored. Carter couldn't tell what bothered him more, the thought of having to re-introduce himself to an old friend ("Hey, I'm Carter Young. Remember?" with an embarrassed smile), or running into someone who still cared enough to demand an account for his absence.

It wasn't that big a deal, he kept telling himself.

� ✻ ✻

It happened within five minutes of his arrival at the plant—he was being led down a cavernous hallway, the thrum of machinery quietly resounding under the fluorescent lights, when he heard a voice behind him—

"Well, Carter Young, how the hell are ya?"

"Hey there .... "

"Darrel. Darrel Morrison; come on, Carter, you remember me."

"Ahhh .... "

"Alright," Darrel patted his ample stomach, "maybe I've changed. So have you, ol' buddy." He gestured at Carter's head, "more than a little gray up top there."

"Oh Christ, Darrel Morrison. Shoot I'm sorry Darrel, it's been so long and all that."

"Yeah, like twenty years or what? It's not fair though, I knew you were comin'. So what are you up to, man? I heard you the new boss now," and Darrel grinned, punching Carter lightly on the shoulder.

"Oh, no, I'm just here to check some things out." Carter looked at his watch, trying to think. They had been friends his senior year in high school; good ones at the time, but Carter couldn't recall the last time he'd seen Darrel other than school. For years, after Carter left for college in Boston, Darrel would call, inviting him back to Luther for parties, a class reunion, a fishing expedition. At first, Carter would politely decline, saying he was just working too hard or that he had other commitments, but promised to drop by soon. And he had meant it too, it was just that things were ... things.

Eventually Darrel stopped calling. Carter was trying to remember if it was for Darrel's wedding that he had RSVP'ed indicating he'd attend, only to change plans without bothering to tell anyone. No point bringing that up now, he thought.

"Yeah, I'm sure you got a lot to do today," Darrel said, "but ah, you wanna catch up later? I'm sure Kathy would love to see you. What're you doin' for dinner?"

Carter didn't even think about it, the words just came out. "Actually Darrel, my schedule's pretty tight. I got a lot of things to go over before I leave tomorrow."

Darrel nodded his head. "Ok. I got it." He turned and started back down the hall. "Nice to see you. And all that."

"Darrel," Carter said, but not very loud, just enough to place it on record. It wasn't anything he had against Darrel; he would probably enjoy a visit. But Carter hadn't yet sorted out his role; he needed to figure out what posture to adopt, what theme to follow. The sheer volume of time measured against these old relationships—Carter didn't know how to address it.

❧ ❧ ❧

The inspection didn't end until 10:00 pm; the Hazmats were outdated and the on-site manager—a kid, really—they got younger every year—was in a talkative mood. Afterwards Carter returned to the room he had booked in Luther's only motel, just outside the village, and lay on his bed, watching T.V. He flicked idly through the channels, pausing at a comically bad preacher who stood motionless at a podium, droning on about Jesus and the scripture's interpretation of modality. A click of the remote and he was watching an infomercial about a revolutionary new "home pastry maker!"—suspiciously similar to a pie plate—with "a dynamic new shape!" (round); "space age construction" (aluminum); and "lightweight design" (again, aluminum). Another channel offered viewers outtakes from c-list celebrity reality meltdown shows, a collection of truly sad moments from desperate people whose humiliations, strangers or no, were too much for Carter to bear.

He went back to the televangelist to try to figure out what he was talking about. He couldn't, but as expected soon drifted to sleep, thinking about how the air smelled so familiar.

—she sat on a metal folding chair in the middle of a small, empty room.

He was standing a few feet away, facing her, as sunlight flooded in through a single window, high on the wall behind him. The shimmering light cast everything in a tinge of gold, reflecting off the walls and the floor to create a haze that clarified only around her.

She was looking at him and smiling, and suffused in the light was the knowledge that she was someone he'd long since forgotten, even though they had once been very close, he was sure. But now he had found her again, and everything was going to be different, he knew, fundamentally better.

Carter was aware that he was dreaming. But the important thing was that he could see her face and he knew her name—not in a conscious sense;

he struggled to bring it to the fore, but it sat buried deep inside him. He just knew that he knew, and all he had to do was pull it from the depths, carry her name out of the dream, or even just the memory of her face, just a shred of her identity to take with him back to the real world and he'd be able to find her, merge the dream with the actual and live both.

Carter focused and tried to commit the slumber shrouded image to memory. But just as he began to mentally grasp it, find a hold and pull her back with him to awake, the light faded and she started to disintegrate. Carter walked towards her, reaching out and prepared to physically take her with him, as if that were possible, and suddenly there was only the empty chair. He stared to cry out—

—and was jolted awake by the electronic warble of the motel phone. "Mmmmph?"

"Your wake-up call, Mr. Young. It's 7:30."

"Right. Thanks."

Carter hung up the phone and fell back to his pillow, staring at the ceiling. Home, he thought. Home. He repeated the word in his head until it lost all meaning.

He got out of bed and pulled on a pair of gray sweatpants that were hanging over the desk chair. Scratching the salt-and-pepper stubble on his chin, he walked to the glass balcony door, stooping slightly as he slid it open and crossed the threshold into the brisk autumn air.

Sun's bright, he thought, but all light and no heat. Carter hugged his arms over his bare chest and shivered, looking at the once-familiar hills surrounding the village. He struggled briefly to recall her name, but gave up; she was gone. It's just a dream, he told himself, there isn't anyone like that who I just plain forgot.

Carter walked back inside. He had a few hours to kill before the flight back, and decided to take the rental and drive around for a bit. Check out the house—years ago he'd heard that the guy who bought it from his folks had painted it red and added a huge addition. Maybe a cruise through the village, let recollection collide with the current, see what change now overlaid his memory.

After a shower he got dressed, pulling on a thick blue sweater and black windbreaker. He had on an old pair of khakis, faded and slightly frayed, and his old hiking boots, worn past their utility for true mountain excursions but still good for a walk through the streets of his youth. After a complimentary cup of coffee in the threadbare motel lobby, he got into the Mercury and drove into the village proper.

Turning onto Main Street, Carter was surprised to find that it was jammed with cars and people. He glanced up and saw a banner strung across the street: "Luther Welcomes You To The 30th Annual Fall Harvest Weekend!"

He had forgotten about that. When he was a kid, the event was held on the village square with six or seven craft booths, a barbecue wagon and a temporary stage for a country band. It was more of a social occasion than a vehicle of commerce.

But now, lining the sidewalks as far as he could see, were vendor stands—everything from custom-made, stainless-steel handcarts that gleamed in the sun to rickety platforms made of bent lawn chairs and scarred two-by-fours. "What the hell," he mumbled, and after several trips down side streets found a place to park.

Walking back to Main Street, Carter pushed into the crowd and let himself be propelled along the sidewalk. It seemed that anything that could conceivably fall under the rubric of "craft" was for sale: hand-knit sweaters, colorful winter caps, homemade hot sauces, antler pot-racks—he took particular notice of some misshapen glass paperweights priced high enough to inform you that the creator intended them to look that way.

Carter stopped to unzip his jacket and noticed that a crowd had gathered to watch a young man demonstrate how to make tulips out of tissue paper and wire. A small bouquet soon took shape in his hands, the brightly colored bits of paper forming cartoonish petals and stalks. Carter was impressed and clapped with the rest of the audience, preparing to come over for a closer inspection, when he saw her out of the corner of his eye.

She was at an adjacent stand, inspecting a jar of maple syrup. As she held it up to the sun he instinctively turned away, wanting to think for a minute. She had gained a little weight, and her once jet-black hair was streaked with gray. But her face, still striking, was unmistakable.

Teresa Harper was his first girlfriend, first love, first everything. They had started going out when he was in 11th grade; she was in 10th. He smiled, thinking how he felt when they walked hand-in-hand down the hall.

They had broken up after three months. For a long time he cringed at the memory, the vicious arguments and petty mind games. Then he got his first divorce, ten years after college. By comparison, he and Teresa's separation was surprisingly adult and amicable.

"Excuse me, dude," said a kid on rollerblades as he bumped past. Jarred back into the present, Carter decided he might as well say hello and picked his way through the crowd to where she was buying two pints of, "Smooth Bark Syrup."

As he approached he could see her fumble through her purse, spilling onto the counter a pack of tissues, keys, a bottle of aspirin, two pens and a vial of prescription pills. The latter slowed him down, he couldn't see what they were but this was not part of the catching up he had in mind.

"Here it is," she said quickly, as if aware of an anxious presence behind her. "I have exact change."

Carter suddenly froze. What was he actually going to say? A nonchalant, "Hey, it's been a long time," seemed too clichéd. She probably wouldn't even remember who he was. Then he'd have to explain ... As Teresa started to turn around, holding the jars in hands more worn than memory allowed, Carter looked away and neatly stepped aside, then watched her disappear into the stream of people. That's it, he thought, time to get going. There were a few places he'd like to see before he left town.

"Carter Young? Sorry, are you Carter Young?"

Carter turned around. "Yes?"

"Hi. Larry Saunders," said a man who was holding out his hand and smiling. He looked about ten years younger than Carter. Red hair atop a wide, square face, short and well built, and dressed in a way that suggested he had made his fortune in a more urban setting.

Here we go, Carter thought, and grasped the hand before him.

"You probably don't remember me," the man named Larry said.

"Um, well .... "

"That's alright, it's been a hell of a long time. I recognized you though." He stood silent for a moment, appraising Carter. "Yup, been a while."

This is going to be bad, thought Carter, I probably ran over his puppy when he was a boy.

"So Larry, I apologize, but I just don't—"

"Well, a long time ago you did me a favor. I always wanted to say thanks."

"What?"

Larry laughed. "I'll bet you thought I was going to try to sell you something. Nope. Just thanks. I mean it, thank you."

"Ok. You're welcome, I guess. And ... for what?"

"Remember Pee-Wee Little League? Christ, I don't know how many years ago, it was the seventies anyway. You were a coach for Robinson's Insurance?"

"I remember coaching." Carter scratched the back of his head to show that he was trying. He had played third base for the school, so when his father's friend needed some help with a little league team, Carter was volunteered. He and a buddy—Darrel?—spent six weeks teaching seventh and eighth graders the basics.

He could remember fragments of that summer, hitting practice grounders and throwing slow, easy-to-hit pitches. But Larry Saunders didn't ring a bell.

"That's ok. I was called, 'Muffin' back then. Kind of overweight, you know?"

Then Carter remembered. A small, round boy with glasses whose parents had bought him an expensive glove and cleats. These accoutrements had little effect on his abilities however, and he didn't seem to have any friends to offer any support. Carter felt sorry for him, and for most of the season stayed after practice to try to help him out.

"I remember, yes," and Carter nodded. "Not that you were ... I mean I remember you."

Larry smiled and shook his head. "Don't worry about it. Listen, you really did a lot for me back then. All that summer you worked with me on my swing."

"Your swing. Yeah, that did need some work."

Larry laughed again. "Well, maybe it didn't help my hitting much. But the thing was, you just spent a lot of time with me." He looked away and his voice dropped. "I was ... the other kids thought I was a loser back then. But you were cool, and you were hanging out with me." He turned back to Carter. "That didn't necessarily make me cool, but they laid off—they couldn't figure out why you did that, but they thought I wasn't so bad then, y'know?"

"Thanks, but I don't think I did anything—"

"No, you did. Sounds kind of strange, it's not like you saved my life or anything. But it was all I needed, a break. I got my act together by the end of that summer. Started working out, lost some weight. Things changed after that. Took a while, but that's when it began."

Carter frowned, opened his mouth, then shut it.

"Hey, don't want to take up your time," Larry said, "gotta go." He looked past Carter and spread his arms. "I've been comin' to this for fifteen years, at least. Gets bigger every year. Anyway, I always figured I'd see you sooner or later. Thanks again though—been meanin' to tell you that for years."

With that, he slapped Carter on the shoulder and walked on.

Carter was stunned. Of all the encounters he had expected, nothing of this nature had crossed his mind. He turned in a slow circle, looking at the crowd with a sudden comprehension. They were all just talking and laughing, strangers and old friends, having a good time on a fall afternoon. No one was judging him—no one ever was, he realized—and the reproach he had carried with him was gone.

"Home," he said aloud.

Then he heard his name again, from a different direction.

"Carter?" Carter Young?"

She was standing behind him, holding out her arms. Without hesitating, Carter walked over and hugged her.

Alicia Cory. All this time and he nailed it right away. It was the smile. They had started dating the summer before he left for college; it ended that Fall on his last day in Luther. He hadn't thought about her in years.

"Carter, I'm so glad to see you! My God, it's been so long! What brings you here?"

"I work for the company that bought the creamery. I had to do some things, flew into Burlington yesterday, heading back in couple of hours. Chicago."

They stepped off the sidewalk onto the grass. "Chicago. I thought I heard that," she said.

"So what's new with you? I mean, in sixty seconds or less?" Carter asked.

Alicia laughed. "Well, the upshot is—"she raised the back of her left hand to his face—"my last name is Richards now, I married ... oh never mind, you don't know him, he moved here a year or so after you left."

"Kids?"

"Randy, and he's in his last year at NYU. Engineering. What about you?"

"Well, no children. But between two divorces I have enough in alimony payments to be raising one, if you know what I mean." The look on her face changed, and he added, "No, it's ok. Things are going really well. I like my job, live in a lakefront condo, drive a new car and vacation in warm places. Things are generally alright. How's that for sixty seconds?"

"Not too bad," and she laughed.

Carter lifted his head, grinning into the sun with his eyes closed. He felt good, and suddenly he glimpsed a room, filled with sunlight and a girl looking at him, smiling. She wasn't Alicia, but he understood, finally, and he knew what to do next.

"Hey 'Licia," the name he used to call her, "please don't take this as inappropriate or anything. But I always wanted to tell you that I miss you." He opened his eyes and faced her again.

Before she could reply, a man's voice called out, "Alicia, come over here, they got those wind chimes we want."

"That's Carl," she said, "Why don't I introduce you?"

"I'm sorry, but I've got to get going. Tell you what though—I think I'm coming back next year for this, so why don't I give you a call then? We'll go out to dinner."

"Promise?"

"You got it."

Alicia paused, then, "You know Carter, I miss you too. Really. Take care of yourself." She hugged him, then turned and walked away.

A breeze asserted itself, strong and noticeably cold. People began to look about, as if reminding themselves that winter was on its way and they should be doing things to prepare. Carter zipped up his jacket and watched Alicia disappear into the crowd. When she was gone, he turned and started towards the car.

He wasn't going to check out his old house or go anywhere else; it was time to head home. He stopped abruptly, held still and closed his eyes as he raised his face to the sun. The girl did not appear. He didn't think she would again.

Carter had the moment—a measure of gratitude and someone who missed him—and he held it tight as he walked back to his car.

Vicious Ghosts

Christ, it makes me wince just to think about it.

❊ ❊ ❊

I was driving home, coming back from a daylong conference at the other end of the state. It had been a long day, and by the time I got on the road, there were only a few hours of daylight left. It was late November, and the frozen landscape was resplendent with the hues of decay—grey sky, yellow grass, black trees. Darkness, I had thought, might be an improvement.

Sitting through six hours of seminars, followed by a monotonous drive through the dead countryside had its effect, and it wasn't long before I started to zone, turning the driving over to a mental autopilot while the rest of me was vacant—lost in the lines on the road, the dimming horizon, the taillights in front of me.

I don't know how long I had been like this when something on the side of the highway broke my concentration. I still can't recall what it was exactly, I passed by too quickly to get more than an impression out of the corner of my eye—a dark fluttering shape, like the beating of large, black wings. I turned to look, but instead of the dark thing all I saw was a road sign, offering directions to my old college.

"Next exit, Tinman State," the sign said.

"2 miles," it added.

Now, I had been back and forth on this stretch of highway at least ten times over the past few years, but I'd never notice that sign before. That seemed odd, and I was also thinking about the strange flapping thing, when suddenly the exit appeared. Without thinking I wheeled over from the far left lane, cutting off a pickup I pretended not to see. Braking hard through the sharp corner of the exit ramp, the car listing heavily as I squealed through the turn, I got that feeling in the pit of my stomach, you know, "this is a mistake." But I ignored this bit of gastrointestinal advice, instead telling myself, "it's been long enough, how can it hurt?"

The classic "note to self:" never ignore your gut instinct.

I hadn't been back to Tinman since graduation, and I never thought I'd return. I hadn't kept up with any of my friends from those days, a mix of intention and a creeping adulthood with too much to drink. It's not that I forgot them, it's just that by the end I wasn't sure which ones I had pissed off for good and which ones got the joke. So I chose the clean break. By the time I felt able to talk to anyone, years later, it had been so long that it'd be a cold call. No more point, you see. They didn't care anymore and neither did I.

Besides, everyone reminded me of Lucy. As soon as I can deal with it, I used to tell myself, I'll get back in touch with some people. But she was the backdrop to every other relationship. Separation was impossible because she was dyed in the fabric of the time. Besides, they would all want to talk about it, and I still can't take that.

So when I left school, I left it all. Moved on, got a job and met someone else. Married, career, etc. And doing pretty well nowadays too. Laying off the booze helps more than I care to think. The only downside of success is that it can highlight former depths.

But there I was, coming back to Tinman on a whim, telling myself that I'd just maybe have a quick drive through, check things out, "for old time's sake." Despite all that had happened, I had a lot of good memories there too, and thought that it might be ok to relive some of those. Just those, though.

Yeah, right. Let me tell you, I have this fucking wonderful capacity to forget ... no, that's not it—to block, to ignore the past, but, like, I know what I'm blocking out, but I pretend I don't. Understand? I don't either, anymore. But I did then. "For old time's sake." My God, I don't even know what the hell that means.

The State University at Tinman anchored one end of the City of Tinman, a once thriving port town located at the juncture of the Fulton River and Lake Erie. In its day, the city was a robust manufacturing center. When I went to school there, you could still see the old factory shells littered about on dead-end streets and along abandoned railroad tracks, gently fading into rusted oblivion.

That hadn't changed.

I was well within the city limits before it hit me. I saw this old cement warehouse, a ruined hulk that canted to one side, its windows long since smashed through. I had no connection to it; was never inside it or anything. But it was one of those things that form a landmark on the mind's map. After leaving the highway, up to that point, I'd driven past a couple of bars I used to go to. Nothing. But when I saw that building, man, I started to feel the old times. And it was just the good vibes; the other stuff hadn't hit.

I kept going, and the geography of the city began to merge with the landscape of my memory. No concrete recollections came to the fore at first, but soon every block had a location that brought back feelings, sort of a reverse deja' vu—I knew I had been there before, but just couldn't quite remember it.

But it wasn't long before some things began to seep through. Another mile went by, and then I saw the diner. Bam—there it was, a clear recollection of the two of us eating lunch there on a hungover Sunday. I had ordered the turkey club and she got a cheeseburger. That look, as she raised it to her mouth, laughing about something I could no longer recall.

It was then, when I thought of Lucy Harker for the first time in years, that it almost ended.

I got so lost in reminiscing that I nearly smacked into a car in front of me that had stopped for a light. I hit the brakes just in time, smashing back into the present but avoiding the car.

All things considered, I can't say if it was bad luck that missed me or bad luck that I missed it.

Shaken, I pulled into a parking lot and told myself to just turn around and get back on the highway. It was starting to snow, coming down heavy, it was almost dark, and home was a few hours drive, doable with a cup of coffee or two.

But some things are never that easy, you know? Decisions that seem so obviously impulsive in hindsight have, at the moment of their conception, an unarguable logic that slips away with time. Anyway, just as I was getting ready to turn around, I looked down the street and saw it.

The Coalbin Tavern sat by the road, about a half-mile ahead. It was an urban island, surrounded by a concrete parking apron on three sides. "Genny" and "Coors" signs hung in the window with electric vigor, suggesting to the young and weary that they need only venture inside to find the Grail. Or several of them.

"Oh hell, why not?" I remember asking myself. "Just one for the road and then I'm outta here. It's been years." And so, without any further consideration (that comes to mind, anyway), I popped the car into gear and drove straight down the hill into the bar's parking lot.

The place hadn't changed much. It was a scruffy, cinderblock box, semi-covered with black paint that was peeling off like tiny, reptilian scales. Nevertheless, for all that it lacked in aesthetic appeal, the Coalbin was a landmark to thousands of Tinman State graduates. With a sharp entrepreneurial eye, the owner of the bar had established himself at a strategic location, to wit: one quarter-mile from the campus, the nearest oasis for the annual arrival of a young, middle class group of kids newly freed of any parental oversight or sense of moderation.

Owning the closest bar to the kids made him a wealthy man, at least it should have, since my attendance alone must've paid the mortgage on the place.

Back in the day, they crammed in as many as could fit. The terribly meek and the hopelessly drunk were pressed up against the walls, unable to squeeze through the mob of people, smoke, and music blasting through the speakers with such force as to become a physical presence. Shit, I remember being stoned in there once and having a conversation with the music. It bought me a beer. On weekend nights, it would be 100 degrees inside, dead in the middle of an upstate January. I'd stare out the window, drenched in sweat and watch the thick snow piling down on cars, swirling about in abstract descents that matched the chaos in my alcohol-soaked head.

I got out of the car and walked to the front door. The snow was already covering the ground. I was startled by a streetlight that suddenly snapped on, casting a pale yellow glow. It actually seemed to make everything in its range darker. I stepped up to the entrance and pulled open the heavy wooden door, pausing at the threshold to look around.

Inside, the place was dim and empty. The bluish glow of television screens provided most of the illumination. It seemed smoky, as if a light fog of cigarette smoke remained from the night before. The sour tinge of post-bottle, floor fermentation lingered about, and I guessed that the place hadn't seen the rough caress of a mop for some time.

The bar itself formed a rather large rectangle in the middle of the room. Liquor bottles were stacked on an inner wooden island next to the cash register and various drinking paraphernalia. The T.V. sets, three facing each long plane, hung from the ceiling above the island. Tables and chairs were scattered throughout the room.

I had my choice of stools surrounding the bar. I picked one in the back that faced the windows so I could see out into the street. Throwing my coat over an adjacent stool, I loosened my tie and sat down, looking over at the bartender. He got the message, and put down a tattered newspaper.

"What's shakin' pal?" he asked.

"Not much. Looks slow today."

"Early still—give it a couple of hours, it'll be packed. What'll ya have?"

"Genny draft. Pint."

He silently poured the glass and set it on a napkin in front of me, then went back to his paper.

I took a gulp of beer and looked around again. The foosball table still sat in the corner shadows by the side door; in the opposite corner sat the pool table. Even from a distance I could see that its green felt cover was torn and stained. The floor around these devices was worn with years of combat, spilled drinks and cigarette ashes.

The beer tasted good. I took another swig, a long, slow guzzle that brought me halfway down the glass. I waited for the burp, felt the rumble and used the extra space to polish it off.

It was so easy. I signaled to the bartender, and he set another cold one in front of me, all the while maintaining a polite silence, as if he understood that a reunion of sorts was taking place.

I took a deep breath, inhaling the fumes like a former smoker taking a long-awaited drag. Picking up my fresh glass, I walked over to the jukebox that sat to one side along the wall. I scanned the titles, looking to see if any of the old tunes were still there. A few that seemed familiar, I lined them up and continued to wander about, stopping now and then to look around or stare at the bar from this angle or that, struggling to recall the circumstances of past visits.

Pint #2 was gone by the time I got halfway around the bar. I made a pit stop for another, completing the circuit while finishing #3.

Let me be clear about this—I had no intention of getting drunk, I wasn't chugging those beers with the goal of getting plastered. I just wasn't paying attention to what I was doing.

Sitting back down in my seat, it occurred to me that this was my usual spot in the old days. A learned behavior, unused for years but never lost, must have taken over and guided me there when I walked in. I grinned, happy in the knowledge that I still had it.

"Hey, another please—when you get a chance."

Pint #4 was deposited on the scarred surface in front of me, and I remember pausing for a moment to reflect upon the contents of the glass. The random patterns of bubbles in flight, the soft shades of yellow and foamy white, the crisp texture as it ran down my throat. And that sour/bitter taste. It was good.

Yeah, only four pints and I got all misty-like about my beer. But even now, there are certain things that I miss—when you get in the right mood, with just the right amount of drink swirling around in your head, and a good tune on the juke ... calm descends, and you just sit and smile.

It would be nice if it just stopped there. If you could safely inhabit that exact buzz for a set amount of time ... But, it seems, you can't.

Lunch at this point was a distant memory, and those four glasses that I poured into my empty stomach began to gain momentum. I could feel their effect, almost imperceptible at first, as an alcohol-laced fog of white noise rolled in, gently obscuring the landmarks of the present, coalescing into a tangible force. Helpless—really, in a sense—I sat there and ordered another beer then another, and another.

I don't know exactly when, but it was probably around #6 that things began to get hinky. The bad memories, the whole point of my exile, began to thaw and cast loose, icebergs adrift in my perception. All that beer ... I didn't just start to remember the past, hell, I tripped and fell into it. I mean, one minute I was sitting there all tipsy and not thinking about anything in particular, and the next thing I know is—

—it's about 10:00 pm and the place is packed. A song is pounding into the crowd, Gregg Allman asking a girl to look at his tattoo. I'm talking to Lucy's best friend, Sarah. The three of us had been whooping it up on the town since noon, and we ended up at the Coalbin. We were propped up against the bar, smoking cigarettes and idly slurring at each other.

Sarah turns to us, and out of the blue says, "You know, you two ought to get married after we graduate."

Lucy and I laugh, but neither one of us says anything. I can tell by the way she is looking at me that she is thinking about it. I get that feeling in my stomach, you know, like, "holy shit, this is real."

I feel really good.

Lucy walks away, mumbling something about finding more smokes. Sarah and I remain to guard our precious barfront property.

"So," Sarah says, "I mean it—wouldn't it be wild if you two got married?"

"Well, I dunno. You think she—"

"Yeah," she says, lifting her glass to examine it. "Lucy would kill me if she knew I told you, but we were talking about it yesterday. She really loves you, Pete."

I'm feeling great now, smiling, just basking in the whole thing. I turned to the bar for another round, I'm going to buy us all another shot and toast to our future—

—the vignette ended. I snapped back to the present, wondering what was going on. The place was starting to fill up, and I was afraid that I might have done something really strange in public. But no one was staring at me, so I just shrugged and kept drinking.

Yup. I should have stopped there; you'd think a minor hallucination would've been a sufficient warning. I can only tell you that it didn't even occur to me to slow down, much less stop. I was on automatic; I just nodded for another round, and there it came.

And I only nodded because I was afraid to verbally order anything for fear that a slurred request would be rejected. That's how drunk I was, I was actually worried that they'd toss me out of that ginmill while I still had money. Hell, I heard of a bartender there who once cut off a paying customer, and he was promptly fired and run out of town.

Another pint was set in front of me. By this time I had lost the dexterity to pull exact change out of my wallet without dropping it, so I just set a pile of cash in front of me, ones mostly, and let the bartender do the work. Then I proceeded to slowly drink it away, a small green hill destroyed by a bubbling flood. The slightly blissful calm gently gave way, and I sat there only numb, watching the faces of past presidents get washed away by glassed waves.

People kept coming into the bar, smoking, talking, drinking, creating the background din that used to be so familiar. But the presence of the crowd only hovered at the edges of my awareness, providing a backdrop for more trips into the past. Support for the lead actors, if you will, because I kept slipping, thinking about old friends.

Jim lived in the room next to mine, in the run-down house we rented with a few other guys. He had a sappy—but to be fair, rather successful—way of hooking up at parties we threw. It always annoyed me; near the end of the night, he'd go into his room and sit in the middle of the floor. He would kill the lights, but leave the door open just enough so someone walking down the hall could see he was there. Cat Stevens would be on the stereo, but the real gimmick was the guitar. The biggest cliché in the world, and it worked great. Jim would be strumming along, sipping his beer (and he always seemed to have another ready for unexpected company) and softly singing along with Cat. The inevitable girl would peek in, go "ohh, what's wrong Jimmy?" and it would be all over. Poor girls, they didn't even know what hit them. I'd see Jim the next day, lying on his bed looking all thoughtful.

"That's so fucking corny, I don't know how you get away with it," I'd tell him. He'd just smile and give me the finger.

"Hey buddy, it works. Try it, I'll let you borrow my Cat Stevens. But you gotta find your own guitar."

But I had my own approach—I just got drunk somewhere and ended up with Lucy.

So there I was, sitting in the bar thinking about Jim and Lucy and Cat Stevens, when I glanced to my left—

—and saw Jimbo at the bar. He was looking back at me, just as the bartender dropped off two handfuls of bottles for us. He winked and waved. I waved back—

—and snapped out of it. Evidently I waved at the bartender, who walked on over, happy to be of service. I think I mumbled something about another round; at least that's what I got.

I knew, in a general sort of way, that it wasn't good to be physically acting out one's memories. But I couldn't really focus on the problem, since the bartender was standing in front of me with an expectant air about him, as if there were some obligation on my part yet to be fulfilled.

I looked down at the bar, and saw that my stack of money had evaporated.

"Ah," I said, hoping he would understand this subtle response as meaning, "no problem, good sir, for I have other means." He looked like a sophisticated sort, and I felt it safe to assume that I was dealing with a gentleman. He patiently waited until I managed to fetch the plastic, despite repeatedly dropping my wallet and knocking over my glass. And the guy's next to me.

You know, bars should require people to check credit cards at the door, like guns and Dobermans. They just don't mix with alcohol.

"Damn the torpedoes and put the whiners belowdecks. Full speed ahead barkeep, and keep a full one in front of me," I said, or meant to, anyway. It probably came out like "'nut her, plea," but he got the message. A cultured lad, like I said.

It sort of gets all jumbled again, but there was a walk to the bathroom that stands out. I don't know why, I'm sure there were many such trips, but I can only recall the one. "Walk" is dignifying it a bit anyway; a controlled lurch would be more accurate. Like saying I "opened" the bathroom door when I'm pretty sure I body-slammed it. I remember hunching down in a corner just past the urinal for a breather; I think I fell asleep for a minute or two.

Wow. And that's not the low point, either.

But I remember thinking that it was refreshing.

Anyway, I was in the bathroom for a while, and by the time I eventually made it back to my seat I was ready for another. God, I remember what I did next—I grabbed my glass, stood on the rungs of the stool, and hoisted my beer, offering a toast to "the good old days." I managed to spill only half the glass on my shirt. Note to myself—open mouth, tip glass. In that order, always.

Despite this faux-pas, I bravely polished off the rest of my drink, climbed back down and looked across the bar—

—and saw Jimbo, Tom, Bobby and Merk standing by the foosball table, looking over at me and waving. Someone yelled, "Where's Lucy?" I looked around, suddenly aware that I hadn't seen her for some time. I turned to ask Sarah where she was—

—and got an elbow in the ribs from some kid screaming at the bartender for a beer. I fell out of my reminiscence, gasping like someone who stumbled into a pit of icy water. For a brief, lucid moment I realized how wildly drunk and out of control I was, and told myself it was time to leave. I'm pretty sure I started to head for the door. But I must've slipped again, because the next thing I know, I'm sitting at a table in the back, this time with a shot and another beer in front of me.

These days I can't even think about that night without shaking my head. Hell, for all I know there were other people already sitting at that table when I plopped down on an empty chair, waving my arms around and mumbling. You ever see a drunk do that, wandering around and talking to himself? I have. I used to wonder why. I figured they were hallucinating, a mix of mental illness and alcohol, maybe some drugs thrown in for good measure.

Now I know what it is. It's not a pure, whiskey-laced craziness. I mean, with most of them at least, things don't just pop into their consciousness and strike up a conversation. No, they're just talking to themselves, to their past, trying to carefully explain to a friend or relative why they zigged when they should have zagged. Put in context, I'll bet the discussions are quite rational.

It's pretty obvious once you've been there yourself.

I got to arguing with Sarah and Jimmy at the table. I tried to justify my actions, explain why I was sitting there with only shades of past friends. I explained that I wasn't mad or too good for them, it was just too much. I had to leave it all behind, couldn't just let go of part and move on with the rest. "It was all or nothing folks. Lucy was all, so I choose nothing."

I knew I had said that out loud, and glanced up to see if anyone heard. Something in one of the windows caught my eye, and when I looked over ... shit, it still gives me chills.

I thought I saw Lucy's face, and those sad, brown eyes staring right at me. I looked around to see if others noticed, but if they did they were pretty cool about it. Then it was gone, but next to me sat Sarah and Jimmy, staring at me just like Lucy was.

That was it. I freaked, started yelling, "Listen, we all drank too much back then. That night. I didn't know. I didn't know. Sarah! You were her best fucking friend and you didn't know either! Jimmy! Where the fuck were you? I'm sorry, I'm so sorry ...."

Some guys at the table next to me had been enjoying my performance. I had noticed them earlier, watching me and grinning, but I was too far gone to stop myself. But then someone said something and they laughed, loud, and it finally sunk in that I was the source of much entertainment. I was not happy with the interruption; it ruined my concentration and caused my friends to scurry back into the dark. I turned to my audience and slurred, "Fuck you, assholes."

They stopped laughing. One of them said something. I didn't hear it clearly, but I got the gist of it.

Things must have escalated from there. I don't recall walking out of the bar, but next thing I remember is standing outside, behind the bar, in a dimly lit corner of the lot. I was facing one of the kids, his buddies stood behind him. A small crowd had formed and a detached part of me noticed that about six inches of snow had fallen on the ground. And I also knew, with that same oddly sober precision, that I had been in this particular corner of the parking lot before. But I pushed the thought out of my mind; I had more immediate problems.

We went through the usual preliminaries of name calling and pushing. I couldn't say much, just another mushed, "fuck you," and a poor attempt at a shove. I couldn't even push that hard for fear of falling over. Then he took a swing and hit me in the stomach. I couldn't breathe and I started feeling nauseous. I took a ponderous step forward, and swung my left fist as hard as I could at the approximate area of his face.

He didn't move. I missed and stumbled forward into him. He just stood there, holding me up and laughing while saying something to his friends. Then the beer and that last shot gave me the coup-de-grace, abruptly unlocking my knees.

I didn't even try to break my fall. I dropped, my face smacking the top of his knee that he had brought up, hard. Boy, I remember that clearly enough. A sharp pain in my mouth, despite the alcohol padding. Turns out that I had bitten the tip of my tongue off. It would look bad and feel worse in the morning.

I hit the ground and lay there, the wind out of my sails, the sails torn down and the masts on fire.

The kid leaned over and started screaming names at me—"crazy old asshole, what the fuck you gettin' drunk here for? Go home, ya fuckin' loser," etc., etc.

Then I felt a lurch in my stomach, and the clot of saliva in the back of my throat told me that I didn't have much time. I got to my hands and knees and lifted my head, feeling the blood, warm and heavy, spreading down my neck.

My counterattack: I leaned forward and threw up on the kid's sneakers. That shut him up; they had been very white, very clean and very expensive, I'm sure.

He kicked me for that, how many times I don't know. I began laughing hysterically, the booze and the pain, the memories of my friends, the memory of Lucy, all mixing inside my head. But it was his last kick that did it, a good shot to the side of my head. Thank God he was wearing only sneakers; puke encrusted as they were, at least they were soft. It almost knocked me out anyway, and I rolled over, face up, staring into the sky, watching the patterns of snowflakes and shooting stars intermingle, drifting to earth or winking out of existence.

That must've been a cute picture—me laying on the snow, covered in blood and vomit, a few feet away the kid and his friends swaggering and jeering, and surrounding us the bar crowd, watching me fade while laughing, talking, drinking.

Well, I had had enough, and just gave it up. I let it all come back.

Lucy was as blind drunk as the rest of us. We had just done a series of tequila shots. God, we were alternating them with small glasses of beer. You know those small glasses they sometimes give you, the eight ouncers? The Coalbin used to give you one of those with your beer if you got there early enough. I still don't know for sure if we had a reason for getting so drunk. Probably Jimmy said something like, "Hey, it's Tuesday."

So we got twisted. It was cold that day—20 below, I think they said later. On the way into town that afternoon, we joked about how if we drank enough, the alcohol would keep us from freezing on the way back.

It doesn't work like that.

They think Lucy was outside at least three hours. The cops, her sister who came up from Pittsburgh, my parents—"But didn't you wonder where she was all that time?" they asked.

No. I just assumed she went outside to throw up, then walked home. Or at least that's what I told them; actually I've asked myself the same question for years.

Later that night, when the lights went on, I stumbled outside and saw all those people running behind the building and I went over to see what was going on.

Sarah is on her knees next to Lucy, crying and holding Lucy's head in her lap. I don't see Jimmy. Then I kneel down next to Sarah and look at Lucy's face.

It is the worst thing I have ever seen. Her skin is white, chalk white. It almost matches the snow she's laying in. And her eyes, wide open, staring, I swear, right at me. I look into those dead eyes and I lose it.

I threw up, started crying, yelling. I don't remember what happened after that. I woke up in the hospital, lashed down with those velcro restraints—they couldn't sedate me 'cause of all the booze, so they just left me there 'til I dried out. Turns out that Jimmy had gone looking for her about half an hour before they found her, but he passed out too. At least he had made it to shelter, some girl's unlocked car. She called the police when she found him and he had to be treated for hypothermia but he was otherwise ok. Physically, anyway.

They next day I left the hospital, caught a ride back to my house, tossed my clothes and stereo into the car, and drove out of Tinman. I more or less got sober, just had one or two every once in a while, just with dinner. And I put Lucy, Sarah, Jimmy and everyone else and everything else associated with Tinman deep down inside, locked, water sealed, and to remain forever undisturbed.

Until I came back.

The kid had given me one last kick, this time in the ribs, and walked away. "You ok, dude?" someone from the crowd asked. I didn't answer. I just lay there, suddenly struck with an idea. It hurt, but I started waving my arms and legs back and forth.

I made a snow angel for Lucy.

When the cops picked me up and walked me to their car, I turned to admire my handiwork—it looked pretty good, except for the blood.

I was taken to the hospital for some stitches on the side of my head, tape on my ribs, not much to do about my tongue. I spent the night in the local jail. No dreams came and I drifted off with a head full of a white buzz that permeated everything. That was a good thing, actually, there's no telling what awful things would have come for me in my sleep.

Waking up in the drunk tank was an unpleasant new experience. The hangover was, naturally, horrific. I didn't just drink too much; I poisoned myself.

Facing a county judge a few hours later was another treat that added a significant degree of embarrassment to the whole ordeal.

I was fined for disorderly conduct. Around noon a cop gave me a ride back to the Coalbin to pick up my car.

It had been towed.

The bar was open, so I went in to ask about the car. Whereupon the bartender informed me that I had yet to sign the credit card receipt for the previous night's boozy seance'.

I eventually got my car back. By the time everything was sorted out it was early evening and I was out over three grand. That was a lot, but I was from out of town. Some things never change.

On the way back I had to stop and pull over twice; I got heart palpitations so bad I was afraid I'd faint.

I told my wife most of the story, the highlights anyway—stopped for one drink, had fifty, got beat up, etc., etc. I left out the part about the hallucinations; she was worried enough about me as it was.

That was some time ago. I haven't drunk much since then. And when I do, it's only during the day, only one, and preferably at or close to noon. I like to have the sun on me, warm and casting no shadows. Sometimes, every great once in a while, I'll toast to Lucy, holding the glass up to the light and looking at a diffused sun through the pale liquid.

But I never stare too long.

They say, "never look back." The cliche' has a nice ring to it, but no one ever explained to me why.

I'll tell you why—if you look back, you might see the ghosts of your past.

If you do, be very careful.

Make eye contact, and they'll kick the shit out of you.

St. John

It was cold, March cold, the gray sky dripping down, wind pushing along the pavement, from nowhere back to same. He shoved his hands deeper into his pockets and kicked the ground, as if to gauge the temperature by the degree of resistance in the broken asphalt. Frank looked down the road again, out along the hazy stretch of Maine's County Route 9 that ran straight on to the Canadian border. He concentrated, squinting at the horizon, knowing it was ridiculous. A car wouldn't appear just from staring and hoping, but he always did watch the pot 'til the water boiled.

A truck suddenly came from behind and roared past. Watching it disappear, he felt a slight pang, wishing that he were inside the cab, moving ahead with clear purpose. And warmth.

He had shocked even himself, just up and said, "Gina, I'm leaving," no expla-
nations, no warnings. She didn't believe him at first, but the scared look on his
face confirmed it and she begged him to stay, actually got on her knees, saying,
"God Frank, I love you, you ...you love me. You said it. What's going on, what's
happening?"

He couldn't answer and was only able to reply, "I gotta go." They'd been living together in Albany, New York, for three years and he had a truckload of stuff
he could claim as his own, but he packed only a duffel bag with some clothes, an
old Walkman and some old tapes; early '80's favorites from high school, leaving
behind the iPod and his cell phone even, going for the clean break, old school.

So he hit the road. He actually walked out of their Hudson Street apartment,
down State Street until he got to the Hilton where he checked in with a stunned
amazement at the dream he was in, only it was real, he was actually doing this. He
threw his bag on the hotel bed and called Kenny, told him to meet at the hotel
bar. He had big news.

Kenny didn't seem to believe him. "Ok, and why?" nodding his head and
rolling his eyes like he already knew.

"I don't know, I'm just—I'm just marking time here, man. I want to head out
and—"

"You want to go looking for Veronica."

Frank narrowed his eyes and looked at Kenny. "What? That's bullshit. That
was so long ago—"

"What's bullshit is that it was so long ago and you're still pining for her. I
don't know what happened, Christ you guys divorced five years ago. You got over
it. I thought. But lately, buddy, every time you get a few beers in you, you get this,
'gotta go, gotta go,' thing going on."

"Yeah, but that's got nothing to do with—"

"Frank, remember last New Year's Eve party? You got drunk and ran into
whats-her-name, Veronica's old friend?"

Frank winced. He had forgotten that. He and Gina had gone out to dinner, a
couple bottles of wine to get into the spirit of things, and he just kept going when
he got to the bash. At some point (it was more than a little hazy) he saw Kathryn
Sears. She used to be a good friend, would go out a lot with him and Veronica,
but he lost touch when Veronica left.

They got talking, and the conversation turned to Veronica. It was a mistake
to ask for her number; Kathryn wouldn't give it to him anyway. A bigger mistake
not to look behind him when he asked, as Gina was standing there waiting to get
his attention.

Kenny had given him a ride home, and Frank had ranted on about Veronica and his life in general. "It's like sleeping on a bad mattress, Ken. I can never quite get comfortable." It was supposed to be deep, but Kenny laughed as he pulled up in front of Frank's apartment. "I'll stick around to see that she lets you in." Gina did, and nothing was ever said between them about it.

"Yo Frank, you there buddy?" Kenny clinked his shot glass against Frank's to bring him back to the hotel bar. "You lookin' a little lost. So where you going?"

"I don't know. Away. Far." He thought for a moment. "North."

Kenny nodded his head. "OK. Here's to North," and they toasted, slamming down the shots. "Waitress!"

❈ ❈ ❈

The hangover from the evening's spree of tequila shots and beer chasers was dissipated with several breakfast screwdrivers. Frank started around 9 am, then followed up with a beer at 11:30. He charged it all to his room, thus stealing it, having no intention of paying the credit card bill. The place wouldn't go under on his alcohol tab, and he needed to save his money anyway.

A few scotches for the post-noon celebration, and he was there. When the buzz hit, it kept the thoughts out, leaving only a purified desire—long since within him but diluted with the tasks of everyday existence—to start running. Somewhere obscure, into the cold and gray, see how far he'd get. No real reason; Kenny was just wrong about Veronica. She was part of it, but only a part. It was something he couldn't shake, a feeling that somehow he was living the wrong fate. He wasn't supposed to be here.

Something went wrong when Veronica left; he knew he couldn't get her back but he shouldn't have just stuck around like he did, going through the motions of moving on, getting a promotion and almost accidentally starting a career as a state employee. More or less ending up in a relationship with Gina who worked in the same office. She was cute and they got along, but there was never the feeling. There was never any feeling about any of it, until lately, and the feeling now was to get away, fast and far. Fast and far.

After an hour of woozily pacing his room on the 15th floor, stopping to stare down at the cars and the people, Frank put his things in his bag and left the hotel, heading for the bus station. He stopped at a convenience store on the way to get a bottle of malt liquor—Colt .45, it just seemed right for the occasion—and a book, science fiction, something he hoped would help him escape while on his escape. But he threw them both out at the bus station; the booze was no longer a good idea, he knew, and the book just seemed—unwise. No more distractions, he decided, he would get on the bus and look at things out the window, at people, natural formations. He would muse on his life, subtly observe his fellow travelers, be friendly to any overtures, all honest replies and thoughtful declarations. He would go, quietly but mindfully, wherever this all took him, as long as it was away.

✖ ✖ ✖

Ten hours and a long nap later, he found himself in Portland, Maine, sitting on an offensively orange-colored plastic chair with a crack in the middle, sipping wretched coffee from a beaten machine in the back and trying to figure out his next move. The bus ride went as planned, numbed observation was maintained, he was simply a biological unit of watching and awareness of events. Chronology, potential, and regret, all were lost, and he was mildly impressed at his ability to achieve this nirvana without the assistance of medicinal distillations.

But Portland was cold. He had worn his black trench coat and knit Giants cap; it was enough for an average Albany winter, but up here it was cold, even in the bus station. He worried about whether he had enough warm clothes. Other than what he had on—blue jeans, a sweatshirt over a plaid blue flannel shirt, Chuck Taylors—all he had packed in the duffel were four pairs of socks and underwear, three t-shirts, a turtleneck sweater, and a shower kit. He could put on his sweater, but then he would have used his last option, and it was too early for that. The sweater would have to be saved for when he really needed it. He couldn't listen to the Walkman; the batteries were dead. Batteries cost money, and shivering in the Portland bus station made him feel vulnerable, afraid that money spent on new batteries would somehow be his downfall; two dollars short for ... something, he didn't know what, but he'd be short and he'd be sorry.

He didn't want to stay here anyway; it wasn't far enough. He walked across the dingy station floor and grabbed a schedule from a scratched plastic case. There were buses heading south to Boston, west to New Hampshire and Vermont, east to Bar Harbor; the only bus going further north was to Bangor. It didn't leave until 4:30 am; giving him a few hours for another nap. He bought a ticket from the woman at the desk then slumped back in his seat, pulling his cap down over his eyes. He used to wonder about people he saw sleeping in bus stations. Maybe they were all like him. Maybe somewhere there was some giant bus station, full of people on spontaneous journeys, waiting on buses to take them to some paradise they couldn't locate exactly but knew was out there, and so they just kept going...

He jerked awake and looked at his watch. The bus was leaving in ten minutes. He was freezing. He got up and shambled to the coffee machine for another cup, wishing he had brought gloves. He went back for his bag, then to the waiting bus, carefully climbing the steps then down the aisle, soaking in its diesel-laced warmth and promise of motion.

They pulled into Bangor at 6:07 am. Wide awake from the coffee and the inevitable stomach-ache, Frank consulted a stained state map on the wall of the Bangor bus station.

"Gateway to the World" a carved wooden sign over the main entrance proclaimed.

He couldn't tell if it was a joke.

Staring at the map, it hit him: he didn't know what he'd do when he got there, but he now had an idea, anyway. The next bus to the border, the town of Calais, didn't leave until noon, but the pain and excitement demanded motion, so he decided to hitch the rest of his way to Canada.

He walked through downtown Bangor, past the same upscale franchises that were in Albany, across the bridge over the Penobscot River, straight into downtown Brewer. Another eleven minutes, passing cheap pizza joints and dollar stores, and he was at the outskirts of Brewer, just like that, no city fading to suburbia fading to country. Just the main street lined with a few brick buildings and a small collection of mobile homes, and then he was alone on County Route 9 in the fuzzy morning light.

He turned, preparing to stick his thumb out, but before he even raised his hand a maroon Buick pulled over and a man who appeared to be in his late 60's, fisherman's sweater and wool cap, just like Mainers are supposed to have, asked him, "You need a ride, son?"

"Sure do," and he got in. The man was going to Mopang Lake, was "just in town to do some shoppin'. Can't beat Wal-Mart, son. Open twenty-four hours, this one. I get in early, I get out early, no crowd, no fuss. Not natural though. May not like 'em—I don't—but can't beat 'em. Get used to it, s'what I say. 'Course, they ever try to put one up on the Mopang and somebody'd burn it, but you live in Bangor you accept these things, I guess."

Mopang Lake, it turned out, was another forty-five minutes down the road. He noticed the lack of any other cars the whole way, and wondered briefly if he had gotten on the wrong road or misunderstood the map.

"I'll drop you off here," the man said as he pulled over just before an intersection. The next town, Wesley, was another 15 miles. "And this ain't no place for someone to just lounge around, son," the man said, not unkindly as his eyes flickered from Frank's cap to his sneakers, "So's you might just want to keep movin' if you can. Get to Canada, some of the bars up there hire barbacks without a lot of questions. The canneries—they're all up the coast—they do too, but them job's harder to get."

"I'm not on the run or anything," Frank replied.

"Right. Here, take this," and the man held out a $20.

Frank didn't want to take it, but he shouldn't have wasted money on the beer and book back in Albany.

"Look, give me your address and I'll—"

"Hey. Don't bother with that. You want help or not?" The man just looked at him, and Frank lowered his eyes as he took the money.

"Ok, maybe not the law, you don't look the type. Not that anyone can tell, at least not me, but anyway. Wife, maybe. Girlfriend. Probably both. Maybe just crazy," causing Frank to look up, "and I don't want to know either. I hit the road once too, ended up in Tulsa." He stared out the window for a moment as the car grizzled quietly by the side of the road, then shook his head. "Shoulda' stayed there, but I thought I was comin' to my senses and came back. Bad move. Been crazy myself ever since." He grinned, but it was a death-row smile, and Frank felt he'd been given a sign.

The man let him out, turned up a pocked side road and rumbled out of sight. All I need is two more kindly old gentlemen, Frank thought, and I'm at the border.

❋ ❋ ❋

Two hours later and he was cold and wet; the damp from standing in the freezing mist had settled in his clothes, sucking the heat from his bones and adding tangible support to the feeling that certain recent decisions may have been poorly made. He had kept walking from where the man dropped him off, turning every few seconds to see if any cars were coming. Only two had. The first was a truck that had roared past, whereupon he learned that the turbulent air of a vehicle's wake is actually much colder than the ambient, no-vehicle air; and a second car that not only didn't slow down, but seemed to actually speed up, the driver, he was convinced, maliciously seeking to induce hypothermia.

He wondered about hypothermia, debated the pros and cons of pulling off his coat to put the sweater on, the ten seconds or so of being colder from no coat for a hopeful payoff of more warmth in five minutes. He stood and stared at the empty road, trying by force of will to bring a car into existence. That didn't work either, and as a last ditch effort, before taking off his coat and trying the sweater option, he sat his bag on the ground and began to do jumping jacks, his breath propelling out white plumes as he jerked up and down.

A few seconds had passed before he realized he was staring at a car, a black compact, coming his way. He stopped jumping and hoped the driver hadn't noticed—though he couldn't see how he or she wouldn't have—and stuck out his thumb. Frank tried to put the right look on his face. Not a happy one, no sane person would be standing out on this godforsaken stretch of highway this early in the morning in the soul-sucking mist and be happy. But grim wasn't good either, even though Frank had the vague impression that Mainers liked grim. He tried to adopt a serene, businesslike posture, that of a man in need of a ride to work or to surprise his long lost Army buddy; the lack of personal transportation a mere inconvenience, a man who was not dangerous in any way and who was not—despite the opinions of old Maine dudes who once were—on the run.

The car slowed, and Frank saw that it was a sedan, a Taurus with Ohio plates. A bright red parking sticker of some sort on the window, and a woman ducking her head to peer out through the passenger window at him. She didn't smile, and Frank had a feeling that she might hit the gas and keep moving. But as she bit her lip and stared, she must've decided that he was ok—she suddenly stopped, nodded her head and leaned over to unlock the door.

Frank pulled the handle and started to get in, but she held out a hand— "where're you goin'?"

He looked at her for a moment, his mind blank. He didn't know how to explain it all within the appropriate time for a roadside encounter, then realized that she wasn't asking for his life story. The bus station map flashed in his mind and he said, "St. John."

She looked up at the road ahead. "How far's that?"

"Well, it's in Canada."

"How far?"

"About one, two hours, I guess."

She looked at him again, checking him out—Frank wished he'd brought his other coat, the blue and red ski-jacket. He had thought the trench would give him a look of respectability, but out here in Fuck All, Maine, he felt like a flasher. He almost reached for his buttons to show that he was clothed underneath, then it occurred to him that this would be exactly the sort of thing a flasher might do right about now.

"Not a flasher," he mumbled.

"What?"

"Sorry. Nothing. Can I have a ride?"

"Get in," she said. "Throw your bag in the back seat."

He pushed a button on the side of the seat and pulled it forward, leaning in and setting his bag next to a cheap suitcase. Then he pulled the seat back, moving slowly, not wanting to appear too eager for fear of scaring her. She looked twitchy. Too eager to flash, he thought to himself and smiled, quickly suppressing it, thinking that anyone who smiled to himself upon entering a stranger's car was surely up to no good. Like a flasher.

The car lurched ahead into the lane, and Frank noticed that the woman didn't even check to see if any other cars were coming. He didn't think it would be good to be critical of her driving this early in the relationship, and sure, it was very unlikely that there were any cars on the road (who knew better than him?), but still. He hoped she was sober.

"Stacie," she said and offered a tight-lipped smile. He took a moment to appraise his driver—late 30's or early 40's, the dark curly hair showing streaks of gray. She was pretty, thick eyebrows arched over brown eyes, thin face and he had noticed a dimple on her right side when she smiled. But her face was hard, too, the smile had faded quickly into an intense stare, a readiness for challenge or confrontation.

She wore a cheap-looking black leather jacket and black nylon slacks atop once-white running shoes. Years of practice performing a quarter-second, descending skim-glance allowed him the observation that she seemed to have average breasts (the slight tautness of the fabric of her white blouse stretched over them), just the hint of a belly. She was short; the seat was all the way up and her legs were straight to the pedals. Perhaps stocky legs, but maybe it was the slacks.

The car was a mess, food wrappers on the floor, hat and gloves on the dash, magazines and empty plastic bags strewn over the back seat, the ashtray overflowing.

"Frank," and he held out his hand to shake.

"So what's in St. John, Frank?" Hers was firm.

Nothing. That was the point, he thought. Hopefully a bar that would hire him to lug bottles up from some dingy basement and wash glasses. A library. A cheap room with, if he was lucky, a view of the sea, but he'd take one that was within walking distance.

"Oh, I got a friend up there."

She looked at him for a moment, then turned back to the road. "You aren't going to try to kidnap me or anything, are you?"

"No. Really. I'm just going to visit a friend. Thanks for the ride."

"Uh huh," she said. "And it's probably just as good that I forget I ever gave you one, right?"

"Look," he said, holding his hands out in front of him as if he were trying to force the point, "I'm not a criminal or whacko or anything. I'm just—"

"You're on the run, buddy. Hell, anyone can see that."

"I'm trying to ... change some things, yes, but nothing like that. What about you anyway," quickly to change the subject, "you from Ohio? I saw the plates."

"Yup."

"Where you heading?"

"You got a sense of humor?"

"What?"

"You got a—"

"Yeah, I guess. But I don't get—"

"Well, maybe I'm going to St. John too. I'd like some company, and I like a sense of humor."

He didn't know what to say to that, and just nodded.

✕ ✕ ✕

After an hour, he knew this: the car had no radio. "Stopped working yesterday. I was drivin' along, hit a bump and it went out, just like that," she told him.

He also knew that the car had a slight shimmy, the right front he believed, and it peaked at around 65. She noticed him checking the speed and said, "I had a boyfriend, he was a state trooper? And he told me that they never stopped anyone under 65 on the highway."

"What state?"

"What?"

"Was he a Maine State Trooper? Or Ohio?"

She was silent for a moment. "Good point," and she slowed the car to 60. The shimmying stopped.

He learned that she liked to chew gum (Big Red), she didn't mind the cold ("I was born in the Northeast, if you're still here at my age you either take it or you're just too dumb to find south"), and she was from Ashtabula, Ohio ("Don't knock Ashtabula—you ever been there?" and when he said no, "Well, I'd tell you all about it but you should see it yourself").

She seemed happy to have company, and although he wanted to sleep, he ended up chatting with her about franchise restaurants ("to be avoided at all costs;

I like to give my money to people, not corporations"), Bob Barker's irreplaceable role in "The Price is Right" ("It was his show, really, I mean who gives a shit how much a box of soap costs, right? But somehow, I dunno, he just kept it, like, interesting"), and the comparative weight-loss benefits of walking vs. running ("don't let them try to sell you some fancy $200 shoes and shorts, you can just walk two miles and do yourself as much good").

She asked him a few more questions about St. John, but his vague responses directed her inquiries to his past.

"Where you from?"

"Albany."

"What do you do?"

"Work for the state."

"Doing?"

"Claims Analyst for Workman's Comp."

"And that entails...."

He smiled. She was persistent. "I spend my day reading comp applications and making sure they fit the requirements for people to get compensated. Like, for example, they actually got hurt, and it happened on the job."

"People file claims even if they didn't get hurt?"

"Well, headaches don't count. Neither does hating your boss, spraining your back shoveling snow so you can get to your job, or getting hurt while on the job, but drunk."

"People actually file claims saying they got drunk on the job and got hurt?" She raised an eyebrow at him.

"You wouldn't believe the stuff I see. I actually like the weird ones, they keep it interesting. I only saw one of those, but yeah, this guy did about seven shots of Sambuca during lunch, then tripped on the way to his desk and whacked his head on a file cabinet. Pretty serious, I guess, gave him permanent black and white vision and he was numb on his butt."

"How serious is that?"

"He wasn't able to tell if he was sitting down, claimed it resulted in an additional back injury from missing a chair he thought was there."

They pondered the meaning of this for a while, until Frank's stomach audibly groaned for food.

She smiled. "I can buy breakfast."

"Umm, sure. But it's not like, y'know, I mean I have money ...."

"I don't mind. I saved up a bit of my P.D.W. money."

Frank squinted and looked at her. "P.D. —"

"Professional Dog Walker."

"Ah … right."

"You know, Joe Lawyer and his girlfriend get a puppy, they work all day, and someone has to take little Foo-Foo for a walk, make sure she's fed, clean the crap off the kitchen floor. Take's fifteen minutes, twenty tops."

"Lot of people pay for that?"

"Nope. But all I needed was five people to sign up. $200 a month, each."

"That's—" Frank hesitated while he tried to do the math, never a skill of his.

"It's $1,000 a month, Frank. That's $12,000 a year. And it's all under the table."

"Yeah, but that's still not—"

"My ex had the job. I stayed at home. Except to walk dogs."

"Oh," and he looked out the window. Thin ice here, and he didn't want to lose the ride.

Imagine that, he thought, I slogged away for 10 years, filling out forms, making sure other forms were filled out correctly, listening to Kenny talk about ultimate frisbee or his long-planned short film, and I could've been walking someone's Rover in my jeans and sweatshirt, a beer with lunch and a nap after, only tough decision is whether to use the rubber glove for Rex's poop or just scoop it up with a paper towel. Gina would've liked it, she always wanted to start our own business, two of us would pull down $24k a year, but no expenses, and if you double the number of pooches—then he stopped the thought. Maybe he'd call Gina when he got settled, now that he was actually under way it seemed ok to back off the "don't look back" philosophy, but he'd have to think about thinking about it later.

"Frank?" She was looking at him closely, "Earth to Frank? You there, buddy?"

"Sure. Just thinking."

"So Frank, you know what else?"

He shrugged his shoulders. "What?"

"Under your seat. The tampon box."

He reached under his seat and pulled out a box of Tampax. "Ok."

"Open it."

He opened the box and pulled out a red rubber-banded brick of twenty dollar bills. "Shit."

"Shit yeah, brother. Breakfast is on me," and suddenly the car swerved to the right, flying into the pot-holed parking lot of a diner surrounded by ruined pick-ups and salt-stained all-wheel drives.

Frank ate the biggest meal he'd had in weeks. His appetite had been diminishing up to his leaving, as if he subconsciously decided to fast before a rite. But now, he was starving—waffles, scrambled eggs and toast with grape jelly, bacon, fried potatoes with ketchup and tabasco, coffee with lots of milk and sugar. Stacie had a cheese omelet with tea, and spent most of her time just looking at Frank. He couldn't tell if it was some sort of come on or if she was debating a fake trip to the bathroom only to get back in the car and bolt. He didn't know how much he cared; he liked her, but if she was going to leave that was fine too, as long as she left his stuff. He thought about asking her what she was planning, but figured he'd wait to see if she got up for a cigarette outside or something like that.

"So Frank."

"Mhmm?"

"I don't know. You really don't mind if I tag along to St. John?"

Your car, he thought, who's tagging along with who? "Not at all."

"How far's the border?"

He stared at the ceiling for a moment as he thought. "I dunno. Probably about fifteen, twenty minutes away."

She looked down into her coffee, then turned back up to face him. "Hey, you want to drive for a while?"

"Sure. You getting tired?"

"Yeah. A little. A meal like this will put me to sleep."

"Yeah, me too."

"But?"

It took him a second. "Right. But I can drive."

"Great."

"No problem."

They were walking out across the parking lot towards the car. The wind greeted him like an old grudge, cutting into his skin destroying the comfortable, sleepy feeling his breakfast had instilled.

"So Stacie, what are you going to do in St. John?"

"What do you mean?"

Frank shrugged. "I mean, you know—you staying for a while?"

"Depends on if I get an invite from someone I like."

He didn't know what to say, but thought he got the gist and pretended to hesitate while he checked his watch and her ass. She whirled suddenly and caught him, but she was smiling.

"Want to stay for a while?" he asked.

"'Bout time," she said.

"Cool."

"Your friend going to mind?"

"Friend?"

"Yeah. You know, the reason you're going to St. John?"

"Right," and he blushed. "No, he won't mind." Frank knew he ought to give it up, she wasn't fooled a bit, but it was just too awkward at the moment.

"And no, by the way," she said.

"No?"

"No."

"No what?"

She raised her eyebrows and shook her head. "No that," she said. "Or at least, don't just assume. It's not polite."

"Not…oh."

"Right."

"Well, hell, I wasn't—"

"I know, if you were like that I'd have thrown you out of the car miles ago. I'm just getting things clear."

"Got it." He did feel a tinge of disappointment, but there was some comfort in subtracting the options. The whole point of the trip was reducing complications, and she was helping keep it simple. Plus, there was more than a hint for the future, and he settled into the driver's seat and started the engine, content in the possibility of intimacy.

✖ ✖ ✖

"Border 8 miles," Frank read the sign aloud as they passed it. They'd been quiet, staring out at the road and the flat, gray landscape. Frank wished it had snowed. He didn't mind the cold, not as long as the sun was out, but the dead grass, dead trees—better to be blanketed with Holy White. Holy White? He worried about his state of mind for a moment. Holy? He wasn't religious. But there was something about snow and silence that seemed reverential to him.

"What do they do, Frank?"

"Who?"

"The border people. Are they police?"

"I guess, why? They make you nervous?"

"A little."

He chuckled. "Don't worry Stacie. They just ask where you're from, where you're going, how long you'll be. No big deal."

"They search the car?"

135

"Not going in. The Canadians never do. The American side does now and then, though."

"How do you know?"

"Back when I was in college, I used to run up to Kingston for beer. Me and a couple of guys; we'd get a few cases, some Cuban cigars, head back to Oswego and have a party."

"Ever get in trouble with the Cuban cigars? You're not supposed to have those, right?"

"They only searched once, and when they found them they gave us a lecture and said they confiscated them. Told us we could get fined for having them, and that next time we'd have to pay a tax on the beer. But as we were driving away, one of the guys gave us a thumbs up and said "have fun." We didn't know what it meant 'til later, my buddy was looking in the glove box for a lighter and found the cigars."

"They put them back?"

"Yeah, the beers were in the trunk, too. They were cool. Don't worry, it's no big deal." He leaned over and gave her shoulder a squeeze, smiling as he shook his head slightly. Gina was like that, always afraid of police or any authority, scared even when going through fire department fundraisers at intersections.

After the usual questions they were waved past the border. Stacie dozed off afterwards, sleeping for half an hour before suddenly sitting up and looking around, a wild look on her face.

"Hey, you ok?" he asked.

"Umm. Little confused, that's all." She blinked and rubbed her face, then, "Where are we?"

"Just rolling into St. John."

She nodded.

"So Stacie," he began, "why are you here?" It seemed a good time to try nail that down, every time he had asked she changed the subject. She looked half-asleep still, maybe this time she'd answer. That, and he needed some time to think; what was he going to do? Where was he going to go? He had only focused on getting here, but the rest of the plan was highly conceptual at best.

Stacie looked out the window, staring at the identical two story wooden houses they slowly passed. Up ahead Frank could see cinderblock warehouses, surrounded by rusting fences, stacks of empty pallets and scattered vehicles.

"Well, Frank, why are you? There's no 'friend' here." She looked around. "There's nothing here."

"Well. I don't know. I think I want to be anonymous for a bit. Just Frank, the guy who works at the bar. Work my eight hours, go home, hot shower and some TV, sleep late in the mornings."

"Go to a diner where they know your name, movies on Saturday nights, long walks on Sunday mornings? Find Cheers and drink with Norm?"

She didn't seem to be sarcastic, so he continued. "Yeah, that sort of thing. People used to go to California, but I'd just as soon go further east. Or north."

"Against the grain. You're a rebel, right Frank?"

This was sarcastic, but not in a mean way and he chuckled with her as they rolled to a stop at a traffic light.

"You know what I mean," he said. "I want to conform so much you can't even see me."

"Then what?"

He didn't know. They sat in silence as the light turned green.

"So you want to know why I'm running Frank?"

He glanced at her, then gunned the car ahead. "Abusive relationship?"

She laughed. "Fuck no. Or at least, not abusive to me. I don't know if I treated him that well." She laughed again.

"So why—"

She lowered her voice. "I stole money Frank. A lot of money. I worked at this company—McGowen Fabricators—they make the metal cases for computers. I was the assistant Comptroller, and one day—two days ago, actually—I just walked down to the bank, told the cashier I need $50,000 from one of the accounts for cash bonuses the company was giving out this year, and walked away with it."

"Jesus." He didn't know what else to say. "The P.D.W. money—"

"It's crap, Frank. My sister did that, that's where I got the idea to say that. I never walked a dog in my life. I got cash in the trunk—in cereal boxes, tampon boxes, lining of a suitcase. I even have some stuffed into an old laptop, the guts pulled out of it, I just snap the keyboard off and you're staring at three piles of fifties."

"Holy Fuck." So he was riding with a fugitive. For a moment an odd chagrin came over him, the thought that even while on the run, doing the most extreme thing he'd ever done, he was still just an amateur, a kid trying to play grown up.

"Stacie—"

"Name's not 'Stacie,' Frank. It's Kim."

He nodded. Made sense. "This your car, Kim?"

She smiled. "Nope. It's rented under the name of Stacie Burrey, of Ashtabula, Ohio. I'm from Jamestown, Frank," anticipating his next question.

"How did you do that?"

"Stacie's a new secretary in the Finance office. Just moved to town. She left her purse at the office the day before I took off; I was working late and borrowed her license and credit card. We don't look much alike, but no one ever questions that. She's probably realized by now it's all missing, but I bet Hertz doesn't know what's up yet. By the time they do, I'll have something else."

"Jesus."

"You sure are religious, Frank."

"'Do you mind driving Frank?', mimicking her voice.' "Right," and he shook his head.

"Yeah, well, I was nervous."

"They got your license info at the border, Sta—Kim. They'll figure it out sooner or later."

She sighed. "I know. Too late now anyway. I think I'll ditch the car somewhere. Get lost somewhere else." She looked around. "I think this town's too small."

"Why did you do it?"

"Why did you leave Albany?"

He thought for a moment. "Right. So, when the police figure it all out, they'll find out I was with you." She started to shake her head, but he interrupted. "They took my license at the border too. They write that stuff down, looking for just this sort of thing."

"I'm sorry," she shook her head. "I shouldn't have picked you up. I shouldn't have told you any of this," and she reached under her seat. For a moment he felt a trill of fear in his stomach. She pulled out an envelope and threw it at him. "Here. It's only $1,000, but it ought to help you get settled in."

"Thanks, Kim. Really, but you need it more than—"

"I got $49,000, Bub. You got nothing."

"Yeah but—"

"And what the hell Frank? I saw that look." She turned to him quickly, a hard look on her face. "You think I was going to pull a gun? Shoot you and leave you in a ditch? I stole some money from a company, Frank, that's all. This your first time in the real world?"

He didn't say anything.

"You're a little old to be in the real world for the first time, Frank."

"Yeah." To his right appeared a view of the harbor, about half a mile off, and he could see a solitary concrete dock jutting into the slate-colored water. There was a forklift on the dock, waiting for a ship. But no people. He looked ahead-the tallest structure seemed to be a four-story concrete office building in what he assumed was the center of town.

"Why don't you just come with me?"

"I don't...I mean, it's just..."

"This isn't a marriage proposal," she said, lighting up a cigarette, "I just don't want to do this alone right now. You seem like a nice guy. What, you had other plans?"

Suddenly he could see the future. They'd be together for six months, maybe a year. Cheap apartments, maybe squatting. He'd work in bars or construction and she'd waitress. He'd fall in love probably, for a while anyway. Then he'd want to settle down. They would eventually part and it would be bittersweet. Perhaps some trouble with the law, but he'd worry about that later.

"Well. I guess I needed a change anyway, right?"

She smiled and gave him a quick kiss on the cheek. "So what do you think we ought to do?"

He thought for a moment. "You had the plan. Ditch the car. Montreal or Quebec." He paused, then, "Quebec. I'll bet they don't care about US police bulletins. At least not those involving embezzlers and rented-car thieves."

She stuck out her lower lip. "Hope so."

They drove to the center of town and stopped at a convenience store. Frank bought a map, water, potato chips, and two large cups of coffee. They stood beside the car for a while, silent, sipping coffee and munching on the chips. Eventually Frank set his coffee on the roof, opened the driver's side door and sat down. He unfolded the map, studying it carefully while Kim leaned on the open door and watched over his shoulder.

"Got a pen?" he asked.

She rummaged in her purse for a moment. "Here."

He traced the route to Quebec, then checked his watch. "Won't get there 'til late, ten or eleven. Can you drive? Let me crash for a while?"

"Sack out, Frank. I like driving." She raised her hands to the sky and stretched while groaning. Pulling himself out of the car, Frank looked down and noticed half a tattoo on the patch of skin between her sock and pant leg. It looked like a spider. He grabbed his coffee, tossed it into a trash can and slumped into the passenger seat.

"Wake me up if you need help," as he reclined the seat all the way back and pulled his trench coat over him like a blanket.

"Don't worry."

Frank drifted off, musing on how fast things change. *This morning I'm alone and cold in Portland, this afternoon I've got a new girlfriend—sort of—and beginning life as a genuine fugitive. Sort of.* Then he was drifting down a road again, but this time he could feel the warmth of the sun.

The truck was hauling a load of winter clothes, heading north to a department store in Fredericton. The driver's name was Tracey. Tracey was twenty-eight years old, from Pike County, Arkansas, and content to be passing his days rushing over concrete. New Brunswick today, Maryland the day after tomorrow. A three-day R & R in Chicago next week with a $600-a-night friend who really was a friend and usually spent the money on dinner and drinks for the two of them. Tracey knew some would think his a superficial life, but most people's lives wouldn't withstand close examination either, and he knew that there was more to come, some good, some bad. Now was the time to recollect, think, and plan. Tracey had his shit together and knew it.

The black eighteen wheeler roared along the highway, 10 miles outside of St. John, the CD playing soft jazz. He automatically hit the left signal and checked the mirror as he guided the truck into the passing lane to get around the black Ford compact, and he glanced down into the car's interior as he drove by.

Woman driving, man sleeping, he thought idly as the truck roared past. The woman was leaning forward, looking straight ahead into the distance, the man sound asleep with a crumpled map on his lap. Tracey knew—he just knew—that there was no radio playing in the car, that the man was dreaming of strange, welcoming places, and that the woman had no plans or goals, other than a hope for a better future. He wished her better things, honked his horn as he pulled ahead, and wondered about the random trajectories of life.

Walking

For the past two years, I've gone looking for my brother Jimmy.

I take a week off from work and fly out to Butte, Montana, then catch a twin prop out to the town of Red Lodge and land on this little dirt strip, hardly big enough for a Volkswagen, much less a plane. From there I take a rental (yes, there's a fleet of four cars at the airport, and I always rent the same beat-up Ford Ranger).

It's about another two hours to the trailhead that leads into the Beartooth Mountains. There's more than one, I'm sure, but I go to the one from where we both set out three years ago. Two years ago—the first anniversary after it happened—I'd hiked for a few days, provisions and tent in my backpack, retracing the steps we took. I took photos of myself and put them on Facebook to let people know I hadn't given up.

Last year I just walked in a few miles with some lunch in a day pack, and read a book on a ledge that overlooked a small creek. Took only a few photos, didn't get into details of the trip.

This year I think I'll just drive out to the trailhead and take a nap in the car. There doesn't seem much sense in doing anything else. Coming here is enough of a ritual.

My employer—a small plastics recycling company in Albany, NY—doesn't mind. Not under the circumstances.

"Do whatever you need to do, Dan. However often you need to do it, for as long as you need to do it." That from my manager, Bill DeWalt. Redundant, but kind. He said that to me when I had first asked for the time off.

"We all hope to God you find him," Bill added.

I thanked him, tears in my eyes, ridiculous in a way, but the sheer emotion of the moment—I'm not made of stone. Numb, maybe, but even that can be overcome, and the catch in Bill's voice did it to me, despite everything else.

Then I was walking away, out of Bill's "office", a glorified cubicle in a forest of them. I passed the copy and fax machines, staring at the striations in the worn brown carpet as I turned the first corner and stopped to listen to Alice, Bill's secretary, say, "He can't possibly be alive. Still? He's froze to death or starved."

There was a quick, harsh, "shhh," from Bill. "Alice. Please. You're right, but he needs to find the body. For closure. His family needs to end this, they can't go through their whole lives wondering."

"Wondering what?" Alice asked, not without a little annoyance in her voice. Clearly, she felt that wondering about anything other than just how dead Jimmy was by now wasted one's time. Sharp one, that Alice. Not someone I'd like to answer to.

"Wondering if he ... I dunno, wandered off somewhere," Bill said. "Maybe living in Phoenix. Became a security guard in Lima. Whatever, Alice, but people hold onto hope in these situations, even when they know there's none left."

"So he needs to stop hoping?" Alice was busting Bill's balls, and I couldn't help from smiling.

"I don't know. Did you get the mail yet?" Bill asked.

I got moving before Alice could see me lurking. It feels like I've been moving ever since.

❊ ❊ ❊

I got the job as a composites engineer for Re-Plastics four years ago. I'd been working for GE in Schenectady, my first gig out of school, but was recruited by a college buddy to Re-Plastics. I moved out of a one-bedroom apartment into a nice little townhouse just off of Lark Street in downtown Albany with my then-girl-friend, now very-ex, Angie.

Angie was an attorney for a small but successful firm that specialized in IT transactions, and between the two of us, we lived pretty well. Dinners out most nights, the tab hardly worth worrying about. New cars (a black Audi for her and a blue Ford Mustang for yours truly), all the right clothes, went to concerts, plays, even squeezed out a vacation in Aruba. And this was just after my first year on the job. Not bad. Not much to worry about.

The trip to Montana with Jimmy came as the result of a Christmas bonus my second year. Very generous. Y'know, most people bitch about their jobs and their pay, but man, it all went well for me. Re-Plastics is a good place to work, good work and good people.

I hadn't done anything with Jimmy in a while, so in a rush of Christmas spirit asked Angie if she minded if I took Jimmy on a trip, instead of the Vegas weekend that she and I had recently talked about.

"No, not at all," she said. "Where are you planning to go?"

"I don't know. We've always talked about a real backpacking trip, a week or so. Maybe out West."

She put her arms around me and kissed me on the forehead.

"Take your brother on a trip. You and I will go to Vegas next year," she said.

"Sounds like a plan," I said.

"He's going to be so excited," she said.

Excited he was. I called him at our folk's house the next day. Jimmy was a senior at Siena, living at home in Troy, and itching to do something interesting before he had to use his four years of accounting classes.

"I can hardly wait!" he said, and for a moment I saw in my mind's eye a young Jimmy, six years old, wanting so bad for Santa to bring him a Transformer for Christmas. When Christmas finally came, he spotted a small box under the tree, in the back next to the wall, wrapped in green paper with black musical notes, and decided it contained Transformers. It was 6:00 am, and we were waiting for Mom and Dad to roust themselves, go through the motions of pretending it was no different than any other morning, raise the level of tension to near explosive force, then suddenly remember that there was something special to do. Dad would say, "Ok fellas, open 'em up," and we'd be off.

That morning Jimmy tore into the package, and sure enough, it was a set of Transformers—Defensor, if I remember correctly, and two others. Just what he wanted, and it wasn't like you hear some people say, possession of the thing is less than the anticipation of it, to own it is to lose it, no, not with Jimmy. He loved them, played with them all the time, shit, that's why I remember Defensor, because it was in his room on his shelf through high school. He acted like it was ironically funny, but I knew, it still made him happy to have it, even years later.

I was happy for him too, really, I mean, Jimmy was my brother, and I cared about him, and if he was happy, well, part of me was happy too, right? But then .... It's hard to describe. They tried so hard, my parents, but they never seemed to be able to get the right thing for me. Not fair judging them like that, I know, it's not like if they asked, "Dan, whatever you want, whatever makes you happy, we'll get it. Just tell us." I'd be paralyzed. I wouldn't fucking know. But they were my parents, it was their job to know. Asking me would be worse, a tacit admission of failure.

They knew they never got anything for me that meant as much as it did for Jimmy. But we never acknowledged it. We just slugged out those Christmases, and soaked up the joy that Jimmy felt when another bullshit toy touched his soul.

"I can hardly wait," the grown-up Jimmy repeated over the phone, "I hear it's beautiful out west."

And I hadn't even told him where we were going, all I had said was that we were going on a trip, and it was my treat.

We met the following Saturday at our apartment. I had wanted to begin planning over some beers at Tess's, the bar down the street, but Angie insisted on having him over for dinner.

I'll never forget that night. I hadn't seen Jimmy in a while, and I was in a really good mood, what with the job going well, the bonus, Angie. Living with her was a dream come true; I'd loved her from when we were freshman at Oneonta. She turned me down when I asked her out my freshman year; she turned me down again my sophomore year. But at the end of that year, at a party just after the last day of finals, I got a kiss that gave me hope all through the summer. Turned out I didn't even need to ask my junior year, she asked me out the second day of classes when I ran into her at the student union, and I floated along nicely for years after. There was a time that I was planning on marrying her.

So we're having dinner, I'm in a good mood, Jimmy's in a good mood—Jimmy was always in a good mood, he was like that, it was one of the things that people always loved about him, the guy was really, seriously, happy. Not crazy, hyper, annoyingly happy or anything like that, but just generally always smiling and laughing, and always acted like every person he met was the exact person he had been wanting to talk to.

Angie too, she was ... vibrant. Laughing, telling stories, listening intently to mine and Jimmy's. She loved them all, even the ones I told twice. I hadn't seen her like that in a long time.

After dinner—sushi and ramen bowls from this Japanese place around the corner—we decided to do some shots. Tequila, Angie's favorite. Jimmy went along for the ride, and pretty soon we were drunk, or "dee runk," as Jimmy liked to call it. I'd had a long week, and when the room began to tilt a bit, I told them I had to lie down. I got up, stumbled into the bedroom and dozed off.

The trip was scheduled for mid-June, so we had six months to plan. Every two or three weeks, we'd meet at this coffee shop on Lark and huddle over a small table figuring out the details.

"Where exactly are we going to go?" he asked at the first meeting.

"I'm thinking about the Beartooth Range, out in Montana," I said.

"Why there?" he asked.

"It's about a thousand square miles of wilderness," I said. "I want to get out there where we are totally alone for a few days. No one else around for miles."

"Great," Jimmy said.

"How long do you want to go for?" I asked. "I was thinking of a week."

"Sounds good to me, Bro." He laughed, then gently punched me in the arm. "If your tired old ass can handle it that long."

"You'd be surprised what I can handle," I said.

We would spend a couple of hours in the cafe, figuring out exactly where we were going, the route we'd take, what supplies we'd need, etc. There was more planning than I had thought.

I ended up making most of the purchases since I had the steady paycheck. By unspoken agreement, Jimmy would end up carrying the slightly heavier load in return.

"You want to invite Angie?" Jimmy asked during one of our meetings.

"I hadn't thought about it," I lied, "Do you?"

He got a little red in the face. "No, whatever, of course not. You know. I thought, ah, I thought—"

"—don't worry about it," I said, laughing. "She wouldn't want to go anyway."

"Right," he said. "Oh yeah, Mom wants to know if your cellphone will work out there. She wants us to call every day."

I rolled my eyes. "Afraid that we'll get eaten by bears? Attacked by savages?"

He chuckled. "Well. You know, she worries."

I threw down a fiver for the coffee and stood up to leave. "She should," I said.

By spring I had researched and purchased all the equipment we'd need: two internal frame backpacks, a three-season, two-man tent, two summer-weight sleeping bags. Jimmy was on his own for hiking boots, or so I told him at first, but a minute later I threw him $60 bucks and told him to get a pair. "That's only half," I said, "you cover the rest and don't spend anything less than $100." Cooking supplies, dried food, a water filter, two compasses, two detailed topo maps, a collapsible steel shovel, hiking shorts, shirts, and socks, and a few hundred other "basic" items we needed for a few days walk in the woods.

"I'll get the weed," Jimmy said with a wink.

✖ ✖ ✖

"Whatever," I said. I only smoked occasionally, usually with Jimmy. "I'll take care of the whiskey."

"That's a done deal, Dan," he said, and slapped my shoulder.

By summer, we had made the flight arrangements and planned the route, a thirty mile trek up to Mystic Lake. I had studied the trails and topography much more than Jimmy, who was relying on me to take care of such details.

I put in a lot of time on the job the weeks before we left. Worked late most nights, didn't get home until 9 or 10 pm. Angie was usually in bed by then, sleeping off the day's activities. Sometimes, earlier in the evening, I'd give her a call, but most of the time she didn't answer. I didn't usually leave a message, but later, after checking her cellphone, she'd see that I had called and would call back, explaining that she was out shopping, or working out, or doing something.

I didn't mind. She needed to do what she could with the time she had.

Just like me.

I look back on that time now, and remember the numbness, the preparation. My whole focus was on that trip; there was only the trip and a blank after.

If I knew then how it would feel to come home without him, would I have still done it?

"He really looks up to you, you know," Angie told me a couple of days before we left. "He's so happy to be doing this with you."

"Well, we have always been close, I suppose," I said. "I look out for him."

"That's sweet," she said, smiling at me.

"And he looks out for me," I said, and kissed her on the forehead as I walked past her into the den, where I had piled the gear for the trip.

The flight out was bad. My stomach was in knots, and security took forever. I was sweating a bit, and Jimmy was all excited and happy and goofy, and the TSA boys must've keyed in on all the odd emotions and gave each of us our own special check over, with a full gutting of our carry-on luggage in addition to having to stand behind a semiprivate curtain for a pat-down, metal wand waving session, and general stern look over, as if one of us might crack and 'fess up the bomb hidden between our toes.

"Jesus," Jimmy said as we got away and were able to head to the gate, "I didn't know they were so ... thorough. This ever happen to you before?"

"Yeah, it happens," I lied. I had flown enough times in the past, and this had never happened before. I sincerely hoped it was not a warning of things to come. It was only as we were walking down the ramp, into the plane itself that I remembered.

"Holy shit," I whispered, "did you bring the weed?"

"In the backpack," he whispered back, "packed inside a liquid soap container."

I paused. "But, um little bro—I don't like to smoke wet, soapy weed. I don't care what the buzz is like."

He rolled his eyes. "Duh. Don't worry, it's double bagged in plastic sandwich bags. Don't worry Dan, it works. It's an old trick."

He didn't get the sarcasm. He never did.

The first leg of the plane flight was eventful. Terrifyingly so. Jimmy thought the whole thing was fun, the fool, he was laughing and shaking his head with every "whump" of the aircraft as it fell fifty feet or so, then smack down hard on a concrete pocket of air. You'd think it was just another amusement ride from the way he acted. Me, I was sweating, nauseous, on the verge of panic, and I just wanted to go home and call the whole thing off. I couldn't even get a drink, because the flight attendants were buckled in. The bad stuff only lasted an hour of the four hour flight to Butte, but it was one of the longest hours of my life.

Odd, when I think about it now: it was the longest hour of that week, despite all that was to occur later.

After changing planes in Butte, our little Beechcraft hoisted us up and out of the small city and over to Red Lodge within another hour. We landed at noon, central time under a clear sky. The airport was tiny, a crude runway next to a bright red brick building that served as the terminal. We taxied up to one of the terminals and after the usual shuffling around to get our luggage from the overhead compartments and standing in line to get off the plane, we soon found ourselves walking through the back parking lot, looking for our rental.

"Christ, it's beautiful out," Jimmy said, staring up at the pale blue heavens.

"Sure is," I mumbled. I was distracted. The heavily taped bubble wrap had somehow come off my backpack during transit, and I was worried that something had either been stolen or fallen out. I didn't want to lose some vital gear and climb all the way to the top of some Godforsaken mountain before I realized it was missing.

"There it is," Jimmy said, pointing to the ten-year-old Ford Ranger. He practically skipped over to it. "Can I drive?"

"Please," I said. "I'd just as soon check out the scenery. What do we have, an hour's drive?"

"More like two," he said as he tossed his pack into the back and held out a hand for mine. "You might want to get some sleep."

I looked at him, perplexed.

"It's not like you slept on the plane," he explained, smiling. "Man, I thought you were going to freak out there for a while."

"Right," I said, reaching for the passenger door, "Sounds like a plan to me."

❋ ❋ ❋

"Yo, big brother," I heard Jimmy say, and I felt a hand on my arm. "Time to get up, dude. We're there. Or here. Whatever."

I lifted my head from the side of the door and blinked. In front of me was a grass and fern-covered slope. The sun was out, and I could hear a bird calling.

"What time is it?" I asked.

"Three-thirty," Jimmy said. "Listen, I thought we'd cook something before we got going. Give us some fuel for the hike."

"Yeah," I said. I was starving. I hadn't eaten that morning, had only a cup of coffee. "Did we bring coffee?" I asked.

"Of course," he said, and got out of the truck, pulled his pack from the back, and pulled out assorted packages that represented the disassembled contents of our portable kitchen and related provisions.

An hour later, we'd polished off some spaghetti with freeze-dried sauce.

"Not bad," I said, "It tasted better than I thought it would."

"How often are we going to be eating freeze-dried stuff?"

I almost said, "Only a night or two," but caught myself. "Four of the five nights. I have something special planned for the last night."

"Cool," he said, and rubbed his hands together. I look back on the moment, at his innocent anticipation of what I was going to bring him, and I almost want to cry.

"Well, let's clean up and get going," I said. Meaning: you clean, I'll look at the map. Jimmy got it, we're brothers and understand how these things work out.

148

Twenty minutes later, we were slowly picking our way along a lightly traveled trail that headed straight up the mountain.

"We'll be going up for the next six miles," I said after a while. I was winded, and wondering how Jimmy was doing.

"Whew," Jimmy replied.

"It shouldn't be too bad. According to the map, the trail's not too steep. Shouldn't be any worse than this."

"Good." He was in decent shape and was several years younger than me to boot. But his back had to be twenty pounds heavier; I lifted it out of the truck myself. I didn't offer to lighten his load however, a deal was a deal.

We stopped to set up camp about three hours later. We found a place where the trail leveled out, not too far from a stream, and proceeded to pitch the tent and heat up a packet of freeze-dried beef stew. The air was getting chilly, and we sat and stared at the flame, an intense blue, emanating from the burner, too tired to talk. After a few minutes, I pulled out two brand new LL Bean fleece sweatshirts and handed one to Jimmy.

"Cool," he said, fondling the soft fabric. "Dan, I just want to thank you again."

"Sure."

"For everything, man. The whole trip."

"Hey," I said. "No big deal. You're my brother. You'd do it for me, right?

He didn't reply at first, just stared out into the twilight. "I'd do anything for you, Dan. It's just .... "

"What?" I asked.

He shook his head. "Never mind. You want to start a fire?"

I nodded.

"I'll look for wood. You get the saw," he said, and got up and walked over to a stand of trees, stooping every now and then to pick up a dead branch.

We had a collapsible saw in my pack. I pulled it out and set it up, then dug out the matches and some fire paste. I was so tired I could have just crawled into my sleeping bag and gone to sleep right there, but Jimmy would want a fire either way, and I knew that I wouldn't mind a few minutes of its warmth, a chance to look at the orange and the yellow and the blue, and try to find my place in them.

He returned a few minutes later with an armful of branches. "Here," he said, dropping them in front of me. "Hey, you didn't dig a pit."

"Sorry," I said. "Look, Jimmy, I'm shot.

"Hey, old man, that's ok," he said, and clapped me on the back. "I'm still young and spry. I'll dig it out. Where's that shovel?"

"In my pack." I watched him pull out the short, black foldable shovel.

"I can't believe you packed this," he said. "This thing isn't made for backpacking, it's for car camping." He juggled it up and down. "It's gotta weigh, what, ten pounds? Half steel too, not even aluminum." He shook his head. "But, I guess it's going to come in handy now, right?"

"Right," I said, staring up at the sky.

He dug, and I somehow found the energy to saw up the branches. Soon we were enjoying a small fire under the Montana sky. Just like in the movies.

The next morning, we got off to a reasonable early start, eight-ish, after a breakfast of freeze-dried omelet and gourmet Italian roast coffee.

"Christ, I'm sore already," I said as I pulled the straps of my pack over my shoulders.

"Yeah," Jimmy said, which surprised me. I figured my comment would generate some more "old man" remarks, but I saw how carefully he put his own pack on, wincing slightly as the weight settled on his back.

"I have some aspirin," I said.

"Good to know," he replied, and started walking up the trail.

I grinned; he wasn't going to give in that easy. He'd let his arms fall off first. Typical Jimmy. He was always competing with me regardless of whether I was even aware of it. For the life of me, I didn't know what I'd done to bring that out in him.

A few hours later, we had lunch just off the trail, on a ledge that offered a spectacular view of a small valley. In the distance we could see a bear picking his way through a field, stopping now and then to sniff or paw at the ground. Suddenly he stood up and looked around. He turned our way and held the pose for a moment, and Jimmy waved.

"Hello, Mr. Bear," he said, and the bear eased back down and continued on his way.

It was amazing, all that open space, and nothing there but a wandering bear. All that room, open to the sun, the empty rustle of wind, no significance, no connection to anything that went on in the larger world, just a place on its own, only to be occasionally observed by hikers who sat and watched an aimless bruin, so far from home.

We hiked for another five and a half hours with only two short breaks.

"What's the rush?" I had asked him, hours ago, when I wanted to rest, but he didn't answer and just kept walking. You can run ... I thought to myself.

I had let him keep going, made myself follow, one step at a time, focusing only on the ground in front of me. It hurt, but I can deal with pain. Did it before the trip, Lord knows, and did it after, and the Devil knows that part. We humped along that Godforsaken, middle-of-nowhere, lame-ass, hick-stupid country mountain trail for another two hours, my shoulders on fire, my knees ready to unhinge, and overall wishing to just close my eyes and drop, but I didn't. I followed Jimmy to where he wanted to go.

Finally, at dusk, he stopped. The trail had leveled out, and a cool breeze hushed across the brush and scrub grass.

"Dan, this is perfect," he said. His voice was distant, like a faint light through the fog, but I got it. It meant I could stop. Take the pack off my back. Lie down. Rest.

But not yet. I had to think. I pulled out my map, the one I had spent many late night hours studying in preparation for the trip. I made a guess as to where we were, then I stared at the ground for another moment. A sigh, and I made my decision.

"Wait," I said. "Let's get off the trail a little ways."

"Why?" He asked.

"I don't want anyone walking by our site in the morning, waking us up. In case we sleep in."

"Dan." Jimmy held his arms out. "Who the hell is going to walk by out here? We are two miles east of Nowhere St. Bumblefuck. There's nobody here."

But I had just started walking, straight off the path, through the knee-high grass towards a stand of pines about a hundred yards away.

"This way. Trust me, little brother," I called over my shoulder. "I read that evergreens keep bugs away. And there will be firewood." To prove the point, I stooped to pick up a stick and waved it at him. "Fire! Jimmy like! Come on."

I kept going until I got to the trees. I was in luck, there was a clearing about ten feet in, and I shrugged off my pack and sat down. Jimmy was following, like I knew he would.

"Well, whoop-de-fuckin'-do," he said when he saw the spot. But then he smiled and said, "Hey, you're right. This is beautiful." He took off his pack and did a slow turn. "Dan, you are indeed the man. I love this place."

Then he was all bouncy, walking around the site, saying things like, "put the tent here," and "fire pit there" but he faded fast, and within a few minutes we were both sitting on the ground, leaning against our backpacks, sharing the flask of Dewar's that I had brought.

"Fuck, I'm tired," he said.

"Me too," I said. "I'll set up the tent. You take it easy."

"Why are you being so nice?" he asked, all mock suspicion.

"I set up tent, you take care of breakfast."

"Deal, bro."

I got up slow, putting a hand to my lower back. I hate to admit it, but I can feel the signs of age, and my lower back is the most prominent reminder of the beginning of a steady deterioration. The fucker just can't handle what it used to. My knees, too, I can feel them, as the lining of youth that protected the joints wears away. Back, knees, and that evening, everything else. It all hurt.

I pulled the tent out of Jimmy's pack. It was getting dark, so I took my back-packer's flashlight out of my pack, strapped it to my head to free my hands, and proceeded to set up the tent. Bone tired and distracted as I was, the task was still easy and within minutes I had it up and ready to go.

I looked over at Jimmy. He had dozed off, his head tilted back on his pack and his mouth open.

Well, I thought to myself, there's no time like the present. Might as well get it over with. I think other clichés went through my head, as if the banality of my thoughts could counter the specific judgment due of my actions.

I pulled the steel shovel out of my back. I wasn't in a rush, he was out cold, so I took my time as I pulled the heavy blade upright so that it ran parallel with the shaft, turning the screw at the base tightly so the blade wouldn't bend when used. I pulled the retractable handle to its full length, then tightened that into position as well.

Then, without any further ado, I stepped around and stood in front of Jimmy, and raised the shovel, ready to hit him so hard his ghost would get a concussion.

These things we do. Evil things, and I am aware of my use of the royal "we". Anyway, just as I was ready to hit him, he opened his eyes and sat up, the fucker, a tear in the right eye, and he was looking at me like he knew all along what I was going to do. And in that brief instant I wondered if that was why he had been walking so fast, why he'd been so intense. He was hoping that we'd get some-where, some destination where it would all be ok between us, forgiveness and redemption all around, and we'd walk out as brothers once again, a new beginning in our future and a firm resolve in our hearts, or some shit like that.

Too late Jimbo, I thought, and hit him in the forehead with the shovel. It knocked him back, but it didn't knock him out like I expected. He fell back on his pack, then sat up again, propped on his elbows, staring at me while blood from the swelling wound on his forehead poured down his face. He had a very specific look, and I'm not talking about any guilty interpretation on my part. Nope, I swear to God, he'd managed to capture a mixture of disbelief and pleading just perfectly. Sort of how he cocked his eyebrows, framed his mouth, and got this special intensity in his eyes.

The blood helped, I suppose.

Fuck pleading. I had a future with Angie. He stole it. The second time I hit him, I did it with feeling, swung hard with my hips, and that shovel blade cracked his skull like the proverbial eggshell, seriously, it felt just like that, a sharp report and a feeling of something giving, and his head walloped down on his backpack, bounced up again, and when he fell back, he was out. Out and Gone. Jimmy's gone to his fucking reward, I thought, and did the other things I had to do.

Angie. This was for that night in my apartment, six months ago, and no doubt many nights before and after.

When I invited him over for dinner and had too much to drink. I passed out, like I said.

Then I woke up again about twenty minutes later, feeling a little nauseous. Not sure I'd throw up, but I figured I'd better get up, walk around maybe, just be ready in case I had to make a sprint to the bathroom. So I walked out of the bedroom, not all that quietly, I didn't think, through the kitchen, and into the darkened living room, where Jimmy and Angie were screwing each other's brains out. It's odd, the details you absorb. Like, I thought how Angie didn't moan like that for me. Either he was that good, or she cared enough to fake that hard. Or how, afterwards, just before I crept back into the bedroom, stomach calm and mind cold, I heard her say, "That's the last time here. At least not when he's here," and that last part said in a way to suggest, well, the whole thing might be a bit wrong, but doing it while I was here, well hey—that was really bad.

Then again, she's a fucking lawyer, and they all can spread evil thinly and shade the layers and call it something else and argue over the particular hue.

They kept it up, of course. Turns out they had a regular Wednesday afternoon gig at some stoner friend of Jimmy's who lived just down the street from our folks. And those weeks before the trip? Oh, I know they picked up the pace, heaven forbid they go a whole week without their regular fuck. I guess it was good that James got as much of that sort of fun in while he could.

But who am I to judge, right? But I don't try to shade my evil. It is what it is, baby.

I pulled a towel out of my pack and wrapped it around his head to keep the blood from draining out all over the place. I got his sleeping bag out of his pack, and with a little more effort than I expected, stuffed him inside it. I took a roll of plastic, ostensibly brought as a ground cloth, and wrapped it around the bag and then took some duct tape from my backpack and taped the shit out of it, making the best seal I could.

I sat down next to him and picked up the flask. I nodded at ol' dead Jim, a toast of sorts, and took another swig. I had some work to do.

I had brought a compass and had spent hours studying a topo map of the area. If I had correctly judged where we were (or, to be technically correct, where I was), it was relatively flat for several miles to the east.

I had been tired, but I wasn't at that moment. Nope, with a little whiskey in my blood, and the vengeance out of it, I felt strong and light and ready to do what I had to do. I folded the shovel and put it in my belt, lifted Jim and threw him over my shoulder, and began a slow walk into the dark field behind the trees.

I don't know how long I walked. It felt like an hour, so it was probably only half an hour at the most. But it was well off the path.

I dropped him in a small depression, in the lee of a huge bush, and began to dig.

The shovel really is multipurpose, I thought. Sorry. Humor, dark as it was, probably wasn't appropriate.

The ground was cooperatively sandy. No roots or rocks to obstruct my little grave-digging project. It took three hours, and I was afraid my flashlight wouldn't last, but in the end, I had dug a good deep hole, and threw James DelRoy Madison, second son of Robert Cooper Madison and Sandra Lorne Madison, nee' Richards, into it. Pulled out a baggie of mothballs that I had stuffed into the thigh pocket of my LL Bean outdoorsman pants, and sprinkled them over the body. They might not keep critters away forever, but it couldn't hurt.

And with no further ceremony I filled the hole, spread the remaining dirt out into the grass as best I could, and trudged back to the camp. Whereupon I crawled into the tent and fell into a very deep and, sorry again, undisturbed sleep.

The rest is details. The next day I hauled our gear a few more miles up the trail, set up a camp for another night, and stomped around a lot to look like two of us had been there. After sitting in front of the morning fire, sipping the remains of my whiskey, I got up and commenced my "rush" back to the truck and the short drive to Red Lodge, where I found the Sheriff and reported my missing brother.

"Christ," I said, shaking my head as the tears ebbed from my eyes, "I was drinking—" the empty flask was, helpfully, stuck in my back pocket at the time— "and I passed out. When I woke up, I dunno, midnight, one o'clock, Jimmy was gone!"

Then the search, a three day affair, where my fear of discovery was mistaken for the tension between hope and despair. Or maybe it really was the tension between hope and despair, they just missed the exact nature of said tension.

Two bad moments: first, when they brought out the dogs on day two. I was afraid they'd find the campsite in the trees (which I had failed to mention and nobody ever asked) then, naturally, they'd sniff their way to Jimmy.

However, the day before, as I was returning to the truck, in a moment of what I can only describe as brilliant inspiration, I had stopped to piss over the area where we initially left the trail. I'll bet that threw the dogs. In any event, their handlers were determined to take them to the spot where I had last "seen" Jim, and naturally, those fool hounds were unable to locate their man.

The other brilliant part: me taking Jimmy's sweaty bandana from his pocket before I stuffed him in the sleeping bag, and wiping it all around the campsite where I had last seen him. I then wiped it up the trail a ways and off into some woods that led to a deep gorge. The dogs fell for it and so no one else ever questioned the theory that he wandered off into the gorge.

The second bad moment: the helicopter on day three. I figured that from the air, the hole I dug and all the dirt I spread around would be easy to spot.

Maybe it should have been, but nobody ever did.

I stayed there another week, in a hotel room in Red Lodge. Talked to a grief counselor for awhile. She was good, I actually felt a little better about it all before I left.

There it is. Oh yeah, it ended with Angie when I got back. I never told her that I knew about her and Jimmy. She was wrecked by the news, and suggested that we live apart for a while, "while we got through this." She left, according to the plan, and never came back.

And even though the sheriff and deputies have long since given up—"he's lost son, sorry," from a kindly old soul who looked just like a western lawman should and who put his hand on my shoulder, wiping a tear from his eye—for appearances sake I think I'll keep up my little pilgrimage west for another year or two. Besides, there's this nice bar just past the airport where I've gotten to know one of the waitresses, Trish. She's very cute, and we spent a rather pleasant half an hour in the cab of my rental truck just before I flew back last year. When we were through, she said, "I really like you, Dan. When you come back, maybe you can stay a while."

"Or you can come east with me," I said, and she hugged me.

So maybe that'll work out. I hope she stays true in the meantime.

Or else.

Just kidding.

The author would like to thank the following:

Nicki Stewart, for everything and everything else and that too (photo credit for "Shreds" and "Turning Dust";

Jim, Laura, Hilda, Rob, Jay and Edie for...well, let's just say a lot

Nicola Coleman, for her editorial effort, patience and overall excellent advice;

Marco Leavitt, for his eye for light, frame and overall cool (photo credit for "Time," "Lost in the Static," "Jack and Diane," "The Kindness of Strangers," "Fall Harvest," "Vicious Ghosts," "St. John" and "Walking");

Frankenfiction, the folks who long ago helped me get much of this right the first time;

Shannon and Isabel Ferguson, Tommy Prato, Tim Bopp and Vicky Henges, Dave Hobbs Kuk, Greg Hoghe, Marianne Reilly, Erin Thomas, Jose Paulino, George Ferro, Johnny Salka, Ale Paulino, Ian Stewart; Marcus Ferguson, Barbara Brabetz, Sciortino's, Pinto and Hobb's, Jessica Pinto, Marcus Epple, Maston Sansom, Mia Stewart ("the best daughter in the world,") The Who, The Kinks, EELS, Wilco, Everclear, Son Volt, The Rolling Stones, The Late, Greats Warren Zevon and Lou Reed; John Mellancamp, Ike Reilly, and a whole bunch of bars best left unmentioned ....

Eileen Sheehan for amazingly meticulous editing and keen sense of humor; Tonya Scanlon Massey for the fantastic author photo; Duncan Crary for getting this whole thing off the ground;

Finally, as best said by Steve Earle: "I got friends that I owe/I ain't namin' names 'cause they know/where they stand."

About the author: Damon Stewart lives in New York's Capital Region. He has published short stories in several literary journals as well as travel and outdoor articles for national and regional magazines and newspapers. He produced a short film, "Shot Through the Heart" and a pilot for a reality series, "The List." He was a finalist in the Fall 2011 Buffalo-Niagara Screenplay Competition, and is seeking publication for a recently completed novel.

Splendiferous Arthropod

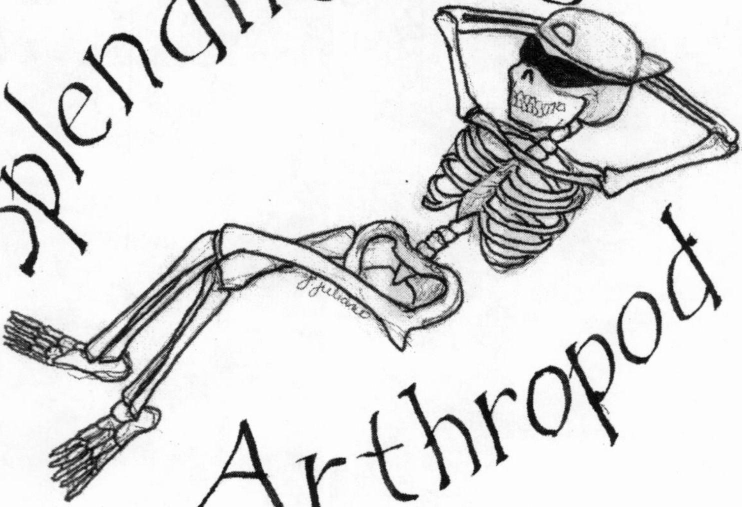

THE PHILOSOPHY OF RELIGION